Gleanings

Gleanings

LOU WILLETT STANEK

HARPER & ROW, PUBLISHERS

Library of Congress Cataloging-in-Publication Data
Stanek, Lou Willett.
    Gleanings.

    Summary: Timid high school freshman Frankie Banning
finds his quiet life turned upside down when a feisty,
adventurous girl moves to his Long Island town and
latches onto him.
    [1. City and town life—Fiction.   2. Long Island
(N.Y.)—Fiction]   I. Title.
PZ7.S78636GL 1985   [Fic]   85-42622
    ISBN 0-06-025808-X
    ISBN 0-06-025809-8 (lib. bdg.)

This one is for my mother, Pearl Willett,
with love.

When thou cuttest down thy harvest in thy field and has forgotten a sheaf in the field, thou shall not go again to fetch it; it shall be for the stranger, for the fatherless, and for the widow; that the Lord thy God may bless thee in all the work of thine hands.

Deuteronomy 24:19

One

The new girl in the class had blue hair! Even Miss Davis, our English teacher who is fairly new in town herself, was looking at this kid like she was a freak. Fallon O'Brien, the prettiest girl in the class, giggled, making it all right for everyone to follow suit. With the whole class snickering, Miss Davis shook her head as if she were coming out of a trance and took the papers out of the blue-haired girl's hand.

She gave us a look and said, "I would like to introduce a new student who has just transferred to us from . . ."

"Mars!" Chub Carruthers said while Miss Davis ran her finger down the page. When Chub can keep the class from hooting and hollering about the layer of blubber he has to carry around, he knows he's on a roll.

". . . Oakland, California," Miss Davis said, "Pepper Marlan who has come all the way . . ."

"Pepper Junior. My name's Pepper Junior." She said it as if she had had the trouble before.

A blue-haired girl named Junior was more than the class could handle. Everyone cracked up. And right on cue, Spike almost tore the door off its hinges and stomped into the room. Until this year Spike had been the football coach, but he had been going down the Island to night school to get his administration degree, so when Mrs. Tishouse retired last year, old Spike traded his whistle for a necktie and became our principal. The kids say he is still a grunt, but I have never heard him myself. I do see him stalking up and down the halls, especially outside new teachers' rooms, just hoping he will find trouble.

Spike stopped dead, like he had been blocked, and slapped a beefy hand across his forehead. "Ohmigod!"

Everybody shut up, not because they took Spike seriously, but because they did not want to miss a word of this scene.

"Mr. Spade, perhaps you didn't have a chance to meet our new student when she checked in with the office," Miss Davis said. "This is Pepper Mar . . . Pepper Junior Marlan from Oakland, California."

"Girl, what in the devil have you done to your hair?"

"Sprayed it with punk paint."

She didn't say it very loud, but she looked him square in the eye. I couldn't help but admire her guts. If I had been her I think I would have quit school five minutes ago, but she hooked her thumbs in the back pocket of her jeans, slumped her shoulders, and kind of rocked as if she heard some music she was keeping time to. She had made a ponytail right on top of her head. About six inches of it stood straight up, but the rest of the icky blue stuff had slipped out of the rubber band and was cascading all around her head with a lot of it flopping around her heavy dark eyebrows. Reminded me of some flowers Mom grows that get straggly and sick-looking at the end of the season. Fallon O'Brien's eyes always remind me of those flowers at their peak.

"Well, go to the gym and wash it out. Right now!" He held the door open. "March!"

Pepper Junior picked up her books and papers slowly. She had a Levi jacket she was trailing on the floor, but she flipped it over her shoulder real jaunty-like before she turned to go. I still can't believe what she did next! I'm staring at her, but so's everybody else. And she winked. At me! I slumped down real quick, thinking it might fly over the top of my head and land on Jeff Porter who sits behind me, but I didn't move fast enough.

"Frankie's got a girl!"

". . . with blue hair!"

"She's got the hots for you, Frankie!"

"Too bad he's a mama's boy!"

Miss Davis saved me when she decided to have us read parts of *Julius Caesar* aloud and cast Chub as Mark Anthony. Everybody seemed to think that was even funnier than watching my ears burn off.

Those guys thinking I'm not interested in girls shows how crazy they are. If I told them some of the things I think about when I try to fall asleep at night, they would blush, and my dad would beat the tar out of me. And Fallon O'Brien's father would send her to a convent. I don't know what's the matter with me lately. It's like my mind has turned trashy and I've got a sewer for a brain. It shames me, and I tell myself I'm not ever going to do it again, but then zingo, the lights go out and those thoughts start popping around in my head. One night I even had to wash the sheet and sleep on a bath towel, just praying the sheet would dry before morning and God wouldn't punish me for such disgusting thoughts.

But I never dream about a girl who looked as if she had dunked her head in a pot of blueberry jam. Her figure wasn't bad, I guess, but having David Bowie's face spread across her chest kind of distracted you from taking much notice. The jeans were faded and pretty worn out, but they fit nice around her behind, and at least she wasn't tall as an Amazon. Mom keeps saying I've been growing a lot myself this year. Really shooting up there, she says. By junior year, she thinks I'll be about Matt Dillon's size, but I doubt it myself.

When the bell rang, I realized I hadn't even listened to Chub's funeral oration. I probably missed the performance of the century, but I had started wondering if Pepper Junior Marlan could be some relation to old Mis' Marlan who lives in that dilapidated house in the woods back of our potato field. Surely not. The place is right on the Sound, and the wind has been beating the bejesus out of it for years. Dad and I go up there after a storm and help the old lady patch things up, but she doesn't seem to have any money to do the repairs that are really needed. Dad says when he bought the rest of the ground from her twenty years ago, he tried to talk her into selling the house since it was so drafty, but she wouldn't hear of letting go of it or the five acres along the shore it sits on. We always wonder how she makes it through the winter. Can't imagine her bringing in another mouth to feed.

Most of the farmers on Long Island had sense enough to build their houses far enough away from the Sound to keep from freezing, but Dad says there never was a Marlan with any common sense. Mis' Marlan's husband was fascinated with the sea. Dad remembers him sitting up there whittling on a piece of wood and watching the water like he expected to walk across the waves. He got himself drowned when he should have been digging his potatoes, the way I heard it. Left her with a boy to raise and not a pot to piss in. They say the boy turned out bad too, but he was long gone in a cloud of rumors before I was even born. Not that anyone has ever told me the whole story, but from what I've been able to pick up, the juiciest rumor involved one of my sisters. Lydia, of course. My folks had four girls before I came along. Lydia's the pretty one. She lives in the next town four miles away where we do our shopping. She's the feisty one too. Considering what I've overheard, if that Marlan boy had a daughter, she would probably have blue hair.

At the end of the day, I didn't dally around but got on the bus early and took a seat near the back. A couple of the guys from my English class ride the bus, but they get off long before we reach the last stop, which is mine. They had probably forgotten all about that girl winking at me, but I didn't want to jog their memories. Besides, from the window I could watch Fallon O'Brien and her friends horse around deciding where they would go to listen to records without her saying I was staring, like she did once. When she used to live in Manhattan and only came out to the Island on weekends and in the summer, I used to spend a lot of time wondering what she was doing. I'm not sure knowing is a heck of a lot better.

The driver had closed the door and hunched forward toward the wheel when Pepper Junior Marlan tapped on the glass and he let her on the bus. She almost looked like a human being with her hair hanging down her back instead of plopped on top like a Zulu queen. It was multicolored like the sweet corn we grow but had some brown and gold sprinkled in too. Streaked like that from the California sun, I guess. Pieces of it curled around her face, which had stripes of blue stuff running clear down to her chin. The gunk she had on her eyes this morning must have melted too when she washed the paint out of her hair, because now she looked like a raccoon I once tried to keep in a cage until his begging eyes made me turn him loose. She had more eyelashes than she needed and eyebrows that looked as if she had glued on a couple of wooly worms. Made her eyes look smudgy as if she had rubbed soot around in them.

She only hesitated in the aisle for a second. I plastered myself against the window and studied a tree as if I were a painter like Fallon's mom, but my luck's always been bad. She headed straight for me.

"When we get home you can go clamming with me at the saltwater pond," she said in lieu of a greeting, as if I had been waiting all day for her to grant me the privilege of wading around in that cold pond my family had owned since the Indians moved out.

No one was saying a word out loud about her sitting next to me, not even Jeff Porter who needs some help from his friends in town to be a bully, but they were nudging each other and I knew who they were whispering about.

"The clams are for chowder, and Granny's making that gingerbread you like. You can stay for supper."

Oh great. We worried about Mis' Marlan having enough to feed herself, and this freaky girl with a face that looked as if she'd been in a fistfight was inviting guests. But how did she know about my taste for gingerbread unless the old lady told her about me making a pig of myself when Dad and I fixed her porch?

"Where'd you come from?" My voice croaks like a frog when I'm uneasy, but she didn't laugh the way some would.

"I've been riding with a bike gang out of Oakland."

Ohmigod! I should've known. I tried not to think what my dad would do if they followed her out here and went roaring down that right-of-way next to our field.

"Is Oakland close to San Francisco?"

"Across the bay. Only Oakland's more chic."

I'd never heard that. My Aunt Gale went to California and came back saying San Francisco was the most beautiful city in America, but Pepper ought to know. She had lived there.

"We had a commune. You know, lots of really tight friends hanging out, doing our thing. Helped each other out. Really cared."

"Didn't your folks mind?"

"I'm illegitimate."

"How can that be? Aren't you Mis' Marlan's son's kid?"

"Who says men make everything legitimate? I don't know who my mother was, except her name was Pepper. Named me Pepper Junior. Put it right on my birth certificate before she split."

Oh terrific! My folks were going to be thrilled when I told them I was having supper with an illegitimate motorcycle queen who might turn up with punk blue hair. I couldn't help feeling sorry for Mis' Marlan. As long as I could remember, she had been holding that five-acre place together with spit, waiting for her son Zack to come back from California like he promised when he went off to make them rich. Some help this dizzy girl who bit her fingernails till they bled and who smelled like a Marlboro cigarette was going to be. Fallon O'Brien painted her nails pink and smelled spicy like a chrysanthemum.

"Where'd your mom go when she split?"

"Hollywood."

"I've never heard of a star named Pepper."

"She promotes rock groups. Makes a ton of dough. She'll probably be coming back to pick me up about the time I go back to Oakland."

"Have you ever seen her?"

"No, we've both been busy. She told my dad she'd have to be moving on after I was born. Because of her career. He promised her he'd look after me until I was old enough to go on the road with her."

I tried to imagine my dad raising me, but that wasn't any easier than trying to erase Mom. Dad was a whiz at raising vegetables and potatoes, but a kid? Forget it.

"Since she's in the business, I get into all the concerts free and stuff. I don't suppose The Police ever get way out here?"

"Well sure they do. Charlie Adams is the state cop . . . and Roy . . ."

She cracked up. Laughed so loud everybody on the bus turned around to stare at her slapping her leg and carrying on like a hyena. I got interested in a fly trying to get out through the back window.

"Oh, Frankie, you're a prize," she said, snorting in a very unlady-like manner, I thought. "I meant a rock group who call themselves The Police."

This crazy girl's conversation was as hard to follow as a scared deer. I don't know why she couldn't just say what she meant, instead of making a guy feel stupid. Dad said he never did meet anyone from California whose head was wrapped very tight. Proved that when they elected Jerry Brown for their governor, he says. Of course, I haven't met Governor Brown myself, but this girl sure is screwy.

"You must've read about their San Francisco concert in the paper. About the dopehead who climbed the flagpole and flew off?"

I didn't want to think about that. I couldn't even stand to look at the rabbits who get run over by cars.

"I was there, and once when I went down to get a Coke I got caught in this crush of people who made a whip and bounced people clear up on the stage. I practically landed right in Sting's arms."

Our bus driver is married to a woman who looks like a hawk, so I've always thought that's why he pokes along like he's in no hurry to get home. When he drew up in front of my house he stopped real slow like usual, but Pepper fell over against my shoulder. Because she's so skinny, I guess. She giggled, and of course my face had to color up like a clown. I got off that bus wondering how I was ever going to make it through eating a meal with a girl who made me as uncomfortable as a tack in my shoe.

TWO

Hitching to school my first day was the right thing to do. Granny would never understand that slinking onto a busload of strange kids was not a sharp way to make an entrance to a new scene. She was right about Frankie Banning though. All the rest of those kids in the English class would have enjoyed seeing that swagger of a principal cut my head off and hang it on the front gate. They were just jealous of my punk paint you sure can't buy in this burg, and here I was washing half a bottle down the stupid school drain. But I could tell Frankie Banning doesn't have a stomach for trouble. Blue eyes turn me on, but it's too bad the only Banning son has to be such a little squirt of a scared rabbit. His old man might be able to fight the summer people and the land developers out of this county, most of which he owns, but they'll trample that kid down like he's a scarecrow. Shows in his eyes.

No, Frankie will never have Rocky Rivers' class act, but he'll have to do. I need him to see me through doing hard time in this crummy school, and I don't plan to hang around long enough to get myself invited into the smart set. Not that I couldn't if I wanted to, but I've got more important matters on my mind. I'll get Granny squared away and be faithful to my true love until Zack's interest in that gold mine starts raining dough, and he can afford for me to come home. Like he said, that crappy room he's sharing with Tick's only temporary. This time he'll probably get us a penthouse with a view of the Golden Gate Bridge. From the San Francisco side! No more walking up alongside an army of roaches. We'll have us a doorman and an elevator when they strike a mother lode. And an exterminator! Some folks pay an arm and a leg for those historic Victorian houses, but Zack and I want something new and zippy with nobody else's grease on the broiler.

I couldn't find a towel in the stupid school locker room this afternoon. Somebody had left a sweatshirt on the bench, so I wrapped my head in that and sat down waiting for it to dry.

I took Rocky's picture and my clipping about The Police concert out of my wallet. I wasn't homesick or anything. Shoot, I knew this year was going to be an adventure. Besides, I'm tough, and a year's not very long. I've already marked eight days off the California Scenes calendar I lifted from the Oakland five-and-ten. Five on the bus getting here, and if this day ever gets over, three on the North Fork of Long Island.

The *San Francisco Chronicle* reporter took a picture of that dopey guy on the flagpole seconds before he took a dive into the concert crowd. I wouldn't have wanted to be around the gory scene when he hit, but I'd rather have gone to that concert than have a one-way confirmed ticket to heaven. I've read the article so many times the ink is wearing off, and I've heard the music on the radio too. Next time there's a concert we'll be able to afford for me to go. Sit right on the front row. The paper calls their music a frenzy. When Zack gets our penthouse, we'll add the album to the big record collection we're going to buy and I'll be able to hear them any time I want to. I'll be older then, and Rocky'll be nuts about me. He'll want to come up and hang out in my room listening to The Police turned up full blast. I'll have a room with a door that closes. No more fold-out couch in the living room. Like Zack says, since I've turned fourteen, it's time I had some privacy. I wouldn't have wanted to live with Tick, even if he *had* liked kids.

I traced my finger down Rocky's sideburns, but a picture—even of a cool guy like Rocky—is slick and cold, and it had turned kind of yellow. But you can still see his cool expression. It's like that Mona Lisa lady that you can't tell if she's smiling or not. One side of Rocky's lip is sort of turned up like one of those smartasses outside the booth at the bus station said something and he's about to sneer. He ripped the sleeves out of his T-shirt so you can see biceps that would make the guys on Muscle Beach eat their hearts out. And he wears those really neat leather bracelets with studs on them. What a hunk!

If he finds another girl this year, I'll bash his head in. Hers too. He won't. He really likes me. Just before I left I could tell he had really begun to change. When I came in the video parlor and those other lunkheads started carrying on about no broads allowed, Rocky never said a word. And he was talking to me a lot more, after that night I took him up to Tick's to get the beer he was dying for.

Zack'll be sending me some bread any day now, but how was he to know what a rip-off those bus stops were going to be. A grilled cheese sandwich costs a fortune. Granny and I are going to eat like queens with all that fish swimming right in front of our door and vegetables growing like weeds all over the place, but I'd rather not have to ask her for money to buy cigarettes and stuff.

When my hair seemed almost dry, I decided to take a walk and have a smoke in peace. I only had five cigarettes left, and I didn't want to chance having someone sneak up on me and make me put it out after I'd only had one drag. Classes were almost over anyway. I'd catch them tomorrow.

As I walked out the back door, it seemed funny to imagine Zack being a kid here, going to school in this same building. He says all the action is over on the South Fork though. A place called the Hamptons, where all the swells from New York come to spend the summer and live it up. Zack says here in Port of Egypt there are just a lot of square truck farmers, potato growers, and fishermen who try to make a guy feel like a piece of shit. When he was telling me what this place was going to be like, he remembered an old girl-friend he hadn't thought about in a long time, Frankie's oldest sister. Lydia Banning was one fun, feisty woman, even though her three sisters could have been missionaries, Zack said, but it would have taken John Paul Getty to have satisfied Lydia. He said her old man was one of the big shots who still thought Port of Egypt was the center of the universe like in whaling days, and nobody was good enough for a daughter of his just because the Bannings had been one of the founding families.

Of course, Zack's luck soured on him here, and then Granny had to sell her farmland to help him out. He's probably just got bad memories. The town didn't look so bad to me, if they'd jazz it up a little bit.

When the mine comes in, the first thing Zack says we're going to do, after we get us some decent digs, is to buy back Granny's land for her. Zack wants to come back here and teach this town a lesson. But frankly, I think he might as well give it up. Granny's a lot older than I thought she'd be. Her spirit is tough as tar, and she's got a lot of spunk, but when she hugs me, her bones feel too close to her skin. Probably I'll take her back to California with me. Buy her a TV, a stereo, and some good records to listen to until I get me a guitar and can play for her. Put her on easy street in the sunshine. I don't think she's up to fussing around with growing potatoes.

After he's had a little Napa Valley red, Zack's always saying if my mother hadn't died, things would have worked out okay for us. Just to show the people around here he could do it, he was planning to come back and buy one of those singles' bars over in the Hamptons where people from New York spend zillions to meet somebody to sleep with during the summer. He was planning on marrying my mother too, but he just hadn't gotten around to it when she had me prematurely and died from kidney poisoning. I believe him because when the hospital found him, he wasn't legally responsible, but he came and picked me up right away. Of course, there was no way a man on his own in California with a tiny baby was going to buy a singles' bar in the Hamptons. Then he met Sue, who had a fetish about not crossing the California border.

I came to the end of the main street, and if I wanted to go any farther I'd have to take a boat. A guy rigging a mast of a tall ship tied up to the pier whistled. I thought about giving him a break, but I would have missed the school bus. Hitching, as I had this morning, would be the pits if I had to do it everyday, so I decided putting off trying the bus wasn't going to make it any more of a roller coaster ride. Besides, I had to continue my campaign with Frankie Banning.

I walked back up the other side of Port of Egypt's main street to see if I had missed anything. No Burger King, no Dairy Queen. Worst of all, not even a pizza parlor! I was half glad not to find a video parlor. Those places inhale your money and don't give a darn thing in return, not even a prize like a ruby ring, but still I'm hooked. Especially on Ms. Pac Man, where I'm really an ace.

A general store with a coffee shop in back, a quilt shop, a historical museum, a clothing store with boring, preppy clothes. Too tame for my taste. Even the post office was in one of those shingled buildings that looked as if it had been there since Columbus landed. Saltboxes, Granny calls them. We live in one, but Granny laughs and says our salt wouldn't pour. It's a little damp. Nice though.

That Banning kid is too much. I got back to school

just as the bus was ready to pull out and when I hopped on, Frankie looked as if he were trying to make himself disappear. So he still plays with marbles—what did he think I was going to do, tell him the facts of life? All I did was wink at him, for heavensakes. I decided as soon as he got to know me, he would realize I was the best thing that ever happened to him, so I sat with him even though he didn't look friendly.

Making conversation with Frankie was as easy as swallowing glass. After a while, I took a rest and looked out the window. We were passing one of the potato fields as boring as the last one when I saw something weird. A grizzly-haired old black man wearing a hunting cap was stealing potatoes in broad daylight. He had a rusty green truck pulled off the road, and he was loading it from a pile of potatoes the farmer had stacked up in the corner of his field. I was sending the old man mental messages to run, thinking maybe he was hard of hearing and didn't realize the bus driver could see him out there plain as a billboard. But when we got up even with him, he tipped his cap. The poor old guy was nuts. Then the driver tooted the horn, and I thought I was crazy.

"What's the matter with you?" Frankie asked, like I was embarrassing him again. "That's Wilbur Brown. Don't they have black people in Oakland, California?"

"Well, of course, they do! But he was obviously stealing those potatoes and not even trying to hide it."

"He wasn't stealing. Didn't you ever hear of gleanings?"

I tossed my hair the way Farrah Fawcett does on TV and said, "I'm not a farmer."

"You've surely read the Bible where it says to leave the gleanings in the field for the poor? Everybody out here does it. Wilbur was just picking up what Vic Terry left for him."

I thought about the wino who used to go through the garbage can back of the bar Zack and I ran for a while. We lived upstairs and I used to watch from our window. But he came at night and kept looking over his shoulder between each bottle he drained.

"Sure we do that in California too. We just call it something different." Frankly, I didn't know what to make of what that Banning kid was telling me. As far as I can see, most people think you're bad if you're unfortunate. I doubted it was much different here, no matter what Frankie Banning said. "But don't you think people feel it's unpatriotic not to be rich? Like if I were poor, which I certainly am not, I wouldn't take anybody's old leftover potatoes."

"I don't think folks feel that way here, Pepper . . ."

"Pepper Junior."

"Mom says its a way of thanking the Lord for giving you plenty and showing your love for other people."

I was glad the bus finally had come to our stop. I

22

wasn't in the mood for this kid to preach me a sermon. To loosen him up a little, I pretended the bus bounced me against his shoulder. All he did was blush, of course.

His house was set back off the road on a lot as big as Oakland City Park and had a huge tree on one side with an umbrella of leaves reaching all the way to the ground. Even if Frankie's pack of older sisters came to stay, that big white frame farmhouse could have held all the Vietnamese orphans as well. On top they had a widow's walk. I imagine they could climb up there and see the Sound. At least Granny and I didn't have to waste our energy on steps. When the tide was in, the water practically splashed in our windows.

Frankie went to tell his mother he was coming to our house, but he didn't ask me to come with him. I didn't care. The yard was interesting with its border of Japanese black pines and a hedge with an arch cut through. The hedge was almost as tall as the house and nearly hid the machine shed filled with funny-looking equipment and a whole herd of trucks. I climbed up on a big tractor and was going to see if I could start it, but Frankie came out before I could figure it out.

"I was thinking about what you said about being rich, but I believe people are more apt not to like you if you aren't sharp than if you're poor."

This kid wasn't too swift. He had better hope for take-home exams.

"Fallon O'Brien's having a Halloween party, and I don't think she's going to ask me." He turned red as a rose, just like when I had winked at him.

"I bet she just forgot, Frankie." Me making excuses for a girl like Fallon O'Brien is the kind of joke that makes you cry, but I couldn't stand to see kids like Frankie feeling left out. "You're kind of quiet, you know? What you've got to do is get her attention. I'll let you borrow my blue punk paint. There's enough left."

"Terrific idea! I'd as soon put a ring in my nose. I'd be mortified."

"Well, we'll think of something else, but if she doesn't remember, who wants to be pestered by parties anyway? You have to thank people's parents and think of ways to get kids to ask you to dance. They're usually a pain."

I didn't know why he cared what Fallon O'Brien thought. Goody Two Shoes. There's always one like her in every school. I had sniffed her out in two seconds. The one the teachers hold up as an example. Boys always make fools of themselves over girls like Fallon who think they're hot stuff. But I'd have thought Frankie would've had better taste.

"Rocky and I'd usually rather just go someplace, like my room, and make out."

"Rocky your boyfriend?"

"Yeah, back in Oakland."

24

After we had filled our bucket with clams, she said we had to go to the beach to collect wood for Granny Marlan's fireplace.

"The beach? Doesn't she buy wood off of Vic Terry?" Every fall he brings us a truckload. Dad says it's worth ninety-eight dollars not to have to break your back in the woods with an ax and a chain saw.

"We could if we wanted to, but we're into saving the environment. Everybody in California knows we're about to use up all the trees. The wood on the beach's already dead and everything."

Looks to me as if Dad would have thought of that, seeing as how he is so concerned about keeping the North Fork the way it is. And picking up wood on the beach isn't as boring as it sounds. That silly Pepper can make about anything seem like a party. She raced around finding pieces shaped like things that made us laugh. I've lived here all my life and I never would have expected to find birds and whales and death masks, but we did.

Pepper went way down the beach and came back dragging a long plank all silvered from the salt.

"Frankie, we'll make two piles. One for the fire and one to build our secret shelter. This board will be the first piece of the floor, and we'll make a stained glass window." Out of her pockets she emptied green and blue and clear hunks of old bottle glass that had washed up on the shore. The rocks had worn the

27

edges smooth, and they were as pretty as jewels, Pepper said.

I had never tried to build a house myself, but she was sure we could do it, so we found a spot in a protected cove and drew the foundation in the sand with a pointed stick.

"We'll live off the sea," she said. "Eat fish and kelp and stuff. But since I'm going to help build the house, you'll have to cook too."

She wrinkled her nose and grinned. Her hair was whipping around in the wind, and her eyes looked shiny and happy with all that paint washed off. I ran off to find another plank because I didn't want her to notice I was blushing thinking she looked pretty. Then too, I had to remember she had a boyfriend named Rocky she made out with in California. But I wouldn't mind if we were just friends. When we were at home. It wouldn't do to have a girl for a friend at school, especially not one as strange as Pepper.

Speaking of boys or girls, I don't have many friends of either persuasion. My folks didn't get around to having me until they were past forty. My sisters were pretty big by then, and so were Mom and Dad's friends' kids. Jack Terry and I used to play together when we were little. Matchbox cars and stuff like that, but we have kind of drifted apart. When he got into hunting, I couldn't see much fun in trying to shoot a squirrel between the eyes, even though my dad says it's a skill every man needs to have. And I like baseball okay, but if half the county—including my family—came to watch, Nick the Greek could take odds on me not being able to hit the ball. So I didn't go out for the team like Jack did even though my dad did some heavy sighing over my decision.

Pepper might be right about Fallon O'Brien not having noticed me yet, but I doubt it. She has to look at the back of my head in history every day. I sit right in front of her and try not to turn around, but you can bet I wash my ears every day without being told. Maybe Fallon is mad because her dad got turned down when he tried to open a wine and cheese bar on Port of Egypt wharf. Dad's on the city council and doesn't like wine or cheese or new businesses.

I found two boards and when I dragged them back to our building site, Pepper had rolled up a tree stump and was perched on it looking out to sea. Sitting on our veranda contemplating the universe, she said.

"We're going to be pals and have scandalous good times, Frankie, you know that?"

She was in such a good mood, I didn't tell her my folks would skin us both if they were too scandalous.

"Now let's go help Granny finish supper. We're having a feast," she said.

What we had was slaw made out of cabbage and peppers from the garden, biscuits, chowder, and gingerbread. No meat or anything, but you know, it did taste like a feast. Seemed like Thanksgiving or Easter. In California I guess they eat most things out of a can because Pepper must have told me twenty times that Granny made everything from scratch.

"No pop-out biscuits or tinny-tasting clams for us, right, Granny?" she kept saying as she jumped around poking the fire and giving us second helpings of everything.

My folks are always worrying about Mis' Marlan, but she seemed fine and dandy to me, maybe because she was so glad to have Pepper living with her. She didn't seem to know much about the bike gangs or the rock concerts.

"She gets her smarts from her daddy, Frankie," Mis' Marlan said when Pepper rigged up a way to drain the dishes into a pan so we wouldn't have to dry them, "but I guess her good looks come from her mother, God rest her soul. No brown eyes in our family. My men both had gray eyes. Bright. Like clouds covering the sun."

I looked at Pepper to see if she was going to mention her mother being in Hollywood instead of heaven, but she darted out the back door to dump the dishwater and then started beating out a rhythm on the galvanized washtub Granny hung on the back porch when she wasn't using it for bathing. Mis' Marlan picked up the corners of her print dress and started sashaying around till the ancient pine floor groaned under what she called her jig. Then Pepper came back, bowed to her grandmother, and they pranced around giggling like a couple of four-year-olds, totally distracting me when they both grabbed a hand and pulled me into their circle. I kicked right along with them just like I knew what I was doing.

When Granny was breathless, she fell into her rocker, but she was still laughing.

"You youngins're going to wear this old lady to a frazzle," she said. "Pepper, why don't you and Frankie climb up in the loft and dig out that chess set your grandpa whittled for Zack. When I catch my breath, I'll pop you some corn out of my garden."

When we got up there, the wind blew our candle out and something swooped right above our heads. I didn't think I'd ever see Pepper afraid of anything, but she screamed and buried her head into my shoulder blade.

"It's just a bat."

The wind had blown away the smell of cigarettes. She smelled salty. Nice.

I was kind of sorry when she grabbed the box and said, "Let's get out of here. Bats give me the creeps."

"Frankie, look how beautiful these pieces are," Pepper said as she started spreading them out on Granny's bright-colored rag rug. "See, the king's a whale and look at this nifty queen. A mermaid. They just freak me out."

She handed me the queen, but I couldn't look at her. That mermaid had breasts and everything.

I had never played chess, and I got a dry feeling in my throat thinking I would look like a dodo, but Pepper explained it so I didn't feel too dumb, even though I think it's probably a game for brains.

"Her daddy was a whiz at that game," Granny said, "but then you know how smart my boy was, Frankie."

Maybe Granny had never heard the stories the rest of us had, or maybe she had forgotten. She was awfully old.

"Seems like them that come late in life always are." She smiled at me like I was just what my dad had ordered, when everybody knows it's Jack Terry with his gun and ball bat Dad thinks is a daisy.

"Your mama and I've often said we had to wait a long time for our boys, but in the long run, God is good. 'Course your mama had her girls to keep her company, but with a farm the size of yours, a boy was what your folks had their hearts set on."

"Don't know why," Pepper said. "Doesn't take a man to run a farm. You just wait and see what I'm going to do to this place, Granny."

"Your coming was an answer to my prayers, honey. And a sacrifice to your father. But then Zack always had a generous nature."

I would have stayed later, since we were so cozy and had such a good conversation going, which is not always so easy. In fact I was thinking maybe Dad was wrong about Mis' Marlan's house being drafty. Couldn't remember when I'd felt as snug. But I had to go to the toilet, and I was too embarrassed to go stumbling around out there in the dark trying to find the outhouse and then come back. They'd have known for sure where I had been, so I said I had better be getting home.

"You want me to walk partway with you, Frankie?" Pepper said.

"No, I know the way."

At night that road is foggy with strange shapes, like Halloween all year round, and I wouldn't have minded company. But I'd have cut off my big toe before I'd have told a girl I walked down that road quaking like a jellyfish.

For the rest of the week, Pepper and I kept that road hot and I got over the surprises it held, but not the ones Pepper was always laying on me.

The next Saturday Pepper and I went with Mom into Blueport, where she does her weekly shopping and visits with my sister Lydia. We horsed around in the library for a while until Jeff Porter and his nerdy friends came in and sat across the table from where I was reading *National Geographic*. At first he started scooting my chair with his battleship boots. I just ignored him, but it made a noise and the librarian gave me a dirty look, while Jeff looked angelic behind his *Sports Illustrated*.

33

I turned a page and just my luck, there was a picture of one of those women from some African tribe wearing only a necklace around her neck. You can bet Jeff Porter wouldn't miss that.

"Hey, Ma'am," he said to the librarian and grabbed the book out of my hand in a flash. "Frankie Banning's looking at pornographic pictures in here. Look at those titties!"

He held it up for her and everybody else to see. I wished lightning would strike him dead.

I saw Pepper dart her head around a bookcase where she was looking for a copy of "The Outcasts of Poker Flats," but then she disappeared.

The librarian had almost finished hissing at both of us when Pepper reappeared and motioned for me to head for the door. I didn't need a formal invitation. Pepper walked behind Jeff, paused for a second, and then sauntered over to the door. Jeff didn't start yelling till we were outside.

"Pepper, what did you do to him?"

I had to run to keep up with her. She was really moving down the street.

"Put two spiders down his back. I found them in the stacks."

She was panting and laughing so hard I thought she was going to choke. When we got to Jake's newsstand and coffee shop, she fell against the wall to catch her breath.

"You got any money? I left mine at home."

"Three dollars," I said.

"Let's get a Coke."

Lots of kids from school hang out at Jake's, but I had never had any business there myself. Pepper marched right in like she held the title to the place. In front there's a cash register surrounded by boxes of candy, gum, and cigarettes, with the magazine racks right next to it. The counter and a few booths are in the back.

"Go on back and get us a booth and a couple of Cokes. I want to look at this magazine," she said.

Jack was working the place alone and he was back at the counter. I told him what we wanted and sat in a seat facing the front, just in time to see Pepper slip a package of cigarettes into her inside pocket. My heart slid up my tongue. Five minutes ago all I had to worry about was Jeff Porter and his friends coming in and pounding us into splinters. Now we were going to have Jake and the cops after us too. Even though I wasn't a regular customer, Jake would be able to identify me. He'd gone out with my sister Ruth for a while.

"Here's your drinks," Jake said to Pepper as she came back to the booth looking as relaxed as boiled noodles. She took them off the counter and slid into the booth where I wasn't breathing. A lady came in to buy a newspaper and Jake went up to take her money. When they got involved in conversation, I finally looked at Pepper.

"Why did you steal those cigarettes? Cripes! I know we're going to jail," I whispered.

"Now, Frankie, don't get so excited. Let me explain it to you."

She put her arms on the table and leaned toward me talking low. Even though she hasn't painted that gunk on her eyes since the first day, Pepper's eyes can still have a raccoon's pleading look.

"They've got some stupid law that won't let kids buy cigarettes, right? Now since I'm addicted and have to have them or I have fits, the only other way would be for Granny to buy them for me, right? Now, Frankie Banning, would you really want a nice lady like my grandmother to ruin her good reputation in this town by having to start buying cigarettes when she's eighty years old?"

"Well, I don't know about the fits, but stealing's not right, Pepper Junior."

"The law's what's not right. When decent people start breaking the rules, it's the rules that are the pits. Think about it."

"I'd like to think about it outside. I'm not thirsty."

I gave her the money. If she thought I was going to look Jake in the eyes, she was crazy. I got outside and leaned up against the wall again, feeling like I'd just escaped from Sing Sing. Pepper chatted with Jake about the weather while he counted the change.

They might think it was a nice day, but I knew better when Fallon O'Brien appeared just as Pepper came out the door and those cigarettes fell out of her pocket and landed right at Fallon's feet. In a bright red package. I darted a look inside and Jake had gone back to washing glasses in the back, but Fallon was still there, right in front of me. I could see her shoes.

Casually, Pepper bent over and picked up the package.

"Hi, Fallon," she said. "I bet you're thinking I smoke those, aren't you, when really we bought them for Frankie's mom."

Mrs. O'Brien works with Mom on the Crusade Against Cancer!

"No, Pepper, as a matter of fact, I don't think about you at all."

"That's good because Frankie and I don't plan to think about you either when we go to this swanky masked ball in Manhattan on Halloween. At the Waldorf Astoria," Pepper said to Fallon's back as she went into Jake's.

"Pepper, why do you tell such lies?"

"They give me hope."

"Hope?"

"If I can imagine them, they could happen."

I was about to tell her if she could manage to get us invited to a shindig at the Waldorf Astoria hotel I didn't think I could handle it, when I noticed the book under her arm.

"Where'd you get that book?"

"The library. Where'd you think?"

"But you didn't have time to check it out! You were too busy catching spiders."

"Frankie, no wonder there's so much suffering and misery in this world. Sometimes it's just not worth the trouble to save people's necks. Here I kept Jeff Porter from killing you, and all you can think about is one dumb library book."

Jeff Porter is a bully, but I don't think he would kill anyone.

"They've got so many books over at that library, they sell some off every Saturday."

She opened the copy of Harte's short stories she hadn't checked out and looked at the charge-out slip.

"Mildred Terry checked this out in June 1979. Doesn't look as if anyone's been standing in line to get their hands on it since."

"Why d'you want to read 'The Outcasts of Poker Flats'? Doesn't sound to me as if it'd have much zip to it."

"It's about gold mining. Since my daddy's in with some guys who're just about to strike it rich, I thought it'd be interesting."

We were walking past the bike shop about then, and she stopped to look in the window.

"When the mine comes in, I'll probably buy one of those ten-speeds, until I'm old enough to drive a Maserati. Zack said in his last letter they'll probably strike the mother lode any day now."

Mom says it's enough to break your heart how Pepper makes two and three trips a day down to their mailbox like maybe she'd overlooked something the first time. The Marlans' box sits on the road right next to ours, and Mom declares Clyde Adams hasn't put a thing in it since Pepper arrived. She thinks it's un-Christian for Zack not to send Pepper money for a warm coat since there's a nip in the air and she's still wearing her Levi jacket. Mom must have missed seeing Clyde the day Zack's letter arrived.

"Does Rocky Rivers write you letters?"

"Sure. Every day. He doesn't know what to do with himself since I left. 'Course, he and Zack realize how nosy rural mail carriers can be. We've made other arrangements. Zack and Rocky and I don't want everyone on the North Fork knowing our business."

My back started to itch, making me mighty uncomfortable. I just knew Pepper had caught Mom watching her out of our kitchen window. Dad says she should tend to her own knitting.

Four

For such a weird kid, Frankie Banning's not so bad. With parents like his, it's a miracle he's not foaming at the mouth. His mother has this habit of chewing the inside of her cheek like it was coated with licorice and she can't stand the taste. She only stops chewing and making funny faces to preach about God or say, "tsk, tsk, children." Calling me a child, when I've had my period for almost a year shows how screwed up she is.

On Friday nights when he stops to drink beer with Vic Terry at The Quiet Man, Mr. Banning is the one she would like to preach at, but like everyone says, he really is the Rock of Gilbraltar. Except for Friday nights, Mr. Banning usually bores Frankie and me to

40

death telling us about hard times when he was a young man. Listening to him, you would think he had to fight ferocious grizzlies and hostile Indians to get down the road to the schoolhouse. Just looking at my face seems to aggravate Mr. Banning, and I don't like it any better when Frankie's mom calls his dad into the kitchen and says, "Now, Frank, you can't blame a child for the sins of her parents. It's not Christian."

Sometimes I wonder if she thinks I don't hear well.

Mr. Banning doesn't care a bit when I hear him say another thing he can thank Zack Marlan for is Mrs. Banning getting herself saved and thinking that church of hers has the answer to everything. I don't have a clue what that is all about. Zack's been mixed up in almost everything, except a church.

Another thing that drives me bananas is having Mrs. Banning watch my every move. Like when I come down to get the mail, if her face weren't framed in that kitchen window, I would think a picture had fallen down. If I didn't know Frankie would catch it, I'd make a shocking face.

The United States government and its inefficient mail system that can't even be depended on to deliver a letter between here and Oakland, California is really what's about to drive me nuts, though. Making transfers in Tucson, St. Louis, and Pittsburgh, I got here in five days on a bus. In three weeks, with airplanes and all, they can't bring me the letters I know Zack and Rocky Rivers have been writing probably almost every day. It's enough to make me turn Communist.

With mail as lousy as it is, Rocky might not have received my address in the letter I sent in care of the video parlor. I was going to ask him for his home address before I left, and then things got messed up and I didn't see him that last day. He probably still hasn't gotten over not being able to tell me goodbye. But living here for nineteen years, Zack sure knows the address. It's the crummy mail system.

Last Saturday when I was coming down the road, I saw Mrs. Banning in the garden taking in the last of the cauliflower, so when I saw the postmaster had screwed up again, I threw a rock at that stupid mailbox. Don't know how she'd gotten to her sentry post so fast, but there she was out on that back porch saying, "Pepper Junior, would you like to come in for some hermits and milk? They're still warm out of the oven, and we've got to fatten you up before winter."

As if cookies and milk could make me forget I didn't know if my daddy were dead or alive. As good-looking as he is, some rich Arab woman could have kidnapped him for her harem. I just never know what's going to happen to Zack. I had some cookies since I didn't want to hurt Mrs. Banning's feelings and those hermits are the best thing I have ever tasted. Granny and I are going to make some as soon as we can remember to buy us some nuts and raisins.

School is easier to put up with than the Bannings, especially Miss Davis, who is not bad for a teacher. Frankie and I have the situation pretty well under control since we are best friends now and can run interference for each other when Frankie can get up the gumption. But that kid can really be a worrywart. Like Monday morning on the school bus. He was *still* thinking Jake might find out about those cigarettes.

"You know, Frankie, I've been thinking that maybe Zack should come out here and marry Miss Davis," I said just to distract him and make him stop bugging me. "She doesn't seem to have a husband or any prospects, and my dad's one sharp man. A real lady-killer. What d'you think?"

"Miss Davis is a real nice lady, but that'd mean you'd have to live with them here in Port of Egypt, and I thought you were just counting the days till you could go back to Oakland. I doubt there's ever going to be a pizza parlor, and you're always talking on about missing Rocky Rivers."

"This place is a drag, and it'd be a big sacrifice, but I suppose for the sake of the family, I could do it."

"What family?"

"Why Miss Davis and Zack and Granny. I think families should hang together. We could fix up Granny's house a little, put a room right up in the attic. Gid rid of those stupid bats and make us real cozy. Teachers probably make a wad of money."

43

"And there's your dad's gold mine."

"Sure. We'd just be rolling in money. Have a lot of parties and stuff. Granny's a regular magician in the kitchen. You can't imagine what she can make out of practically nothing. And because you've been my pal, Frankie, I'll even invite Fallon O'Brien to the parties."

"Oh, you don't have to do that, Pepper Junior. I think Fallon's going with Jack Terry anyway. With you there, it'll be lively enough for me."

In history we're studying explorers, and I already know about Henry Hudson ripping off the Indians and that stuff, so I didn't bother to go. I had found a nifty place in the boiler room where I could have a smoke and some privacy. I had to plan my strategy for getting Zack and Miss Davis married.

Sometimes fate seems to be playing on my team. I went to English class, of course, and Miss Davis gave us an assignment to write an essay about the most unforgettable person we had ever met. What a stroke of luck! I'd write an essay about Zack that would tempt a nun.

"Miss Davis, could that paper be about a member of our family?"

"If the most unforgettable person you know is a member of your family, that would be fine, Pepper Junior."

"My dad's quite a guy. Good-looking. Single. Women

are always just dying for him, but he likes literary types. Ones who read poetry and know a lot about *Great Expectations*. You know what I mean?"

I think she did because her face flushed a little bit and she closed her notebook that was filled up with what she knew about *Great Expectations*. She pretended she didn't even hear the stupid things Jeff Porter and Chub Carruthers were saying about my dad. She asked Fallon to start reading chapter ten aloud to the class.

I heard Jeff asking if Zack had blue hair and worse things about his women friends, but I didn't pay any attention to him—I was already trying to plan my essay. To tell the truth, I really couldn't keep my mind on it. I kept thinking how super it would be at Christmas and Thanksgiving when the whole family gathered around a big old fat turkey. The Bannings would probably all come to eat with us when Miss Davis was my mom. Maybe we would take turns going to each other's houses because there would be lots of holidays since we would never be moving on. No sir. Zack, Miss Davis, Granny, and I would just spend the rest of our lives right there on Long Island Sound. Frankie and I would be best friends forever. I could have had lots of best friends before if Zack and I could have hung around in one place long enough. Like Sandy Porter in San Jose. She was going to invite me to her birthday party at the skating rink and to sleep over if Zack hadn't broken up with Molly. I told Molly I understood why she had to ask us to move out. Like she said, Zack couldn't expect to hang the clothes he was wearing to see Barbara in Molly's closet. But I did miss Sandy Porter.

Going home on the bus that night, I wanted to talk about my campaign to get Zack and Miss Davis married, but Frankie couldn't think about anything but the party he and I were planning to throw in our beach house on Halloween night.

"Since it's just going to be you and me, Pepper Junior, I don't really see why we have to wear costumes. I'll know who you are, no matter how much you dress up, and I'm going to feel plain silly."

"Gimme a break! Who ever heard of going to a Halloween party in your regular clothes? It wouldn't be proper. Granny and I carved the pumpkins last night. You bring the candles. And I picked up apples from under Vic Terry's trees. They were just going to waste. If your mom has some sugar, Granny will make the taffy to coat them. We forgot to get some this week."

When we got off the bus, Frankie went on home, and I stopped at the mailbox, even though I knew the crummy government probably still wouldn't have delivered my mail to me like it should have. When I opened that box and saw a letter in Zack's handwriting, I couldn't have been any happier if it were a stack of million-dollar bills. Mr. Banning had shoved a big

46

boulder out of his field right next to the mailbox. I climbed right up on it and started to read my letter. I couldn't wait until I got home. I'd read it again to Granny.

A ten-dollar bill fluttered out when I unfolded the pages. I looked to see if any more had stuck in the envelope. Well, ten dollars would stretch pretty far the way Granny manages.

On the first page Zack told me again how sorry he was he had to send me out here and how much he missed my funny face, but how he thought it would be good for me to get to know my grandmother. My eyes skipped down and I saw Rocky Rivers' name, so I jumped to that part.

Bea and I really enjoyed all of your letters. [Ohoh, who's Bea?] I've been meaning to get around to writing you sooner, but since you keep asking about Rocky Rivers, I wanted to get back over to the old neighborhood and see if I could find out what he was up to—I've been spending a lot of time at Bea's—He must have been one of those guys you picked up over at the video parlor where you used to spend all my bread, [ha, ha] because I can't place him. Bea and I went to the flicks over there the other night, and some guy I think you brought up to Tick's once was sitting in front of us. Surely wasn't Rocky Rivers though. This young stud with long sideburns was all over some blonde.

He had leather bracelets with studs that kept getting tangled in her hair. Bea and I got a kick out of them taking a breather and trying to get her hair loose.

Sharing that room with Tick is not working out, but we knew what a hardass guy he was when he didn't want you around. But I think you're really going to like Bea. She's a little older, but still a looker and better established, if you know what I mean. Good firm jugs and a tight ass. Her ex-husband left her this little house over in North Oakland. Free and clear. A pickup in damn good condition. I can teach you to drive. She's got a couple of kids, but like she says, thank god they're grown and gone. I think you and Bea will really get along, her having had some experience as a mother and all. Since she just got rid of hers and would like a breather, she thinks we should try it together for awhile before we send for you, but if this works out it could be a really good deal for us. I've explained you're my sidekick. Hell, your old man might even finally settle down. Tie the old knot. What would you think of that? You've always been trying to get us stuck in one spot. Ole Bea's house just might be the place.

Damn him! Sometimes I could just throttle that Zack, I really could. My nose was running, and I couldn't see to read the rest of his stupid letter. He promised me we wouldn't even try to live with any more of his lady friends. It never did work out, even with Molly, and she had liked me. And he's so forgetful, he can't even remember what Rocky Rivers looks like. How could he have recognized him in a dark theater. That wasn't Rocky! I know that for sure. Zack only saw the back of his head. And he's nuts to even imagine I'll like old tight-assed Bea and her house in crummy North Oakland. If he thinks I'm leaving Port of Egypt where everything is nice and going to live there, he's crazy!

I wiped my eyes and my nose on my David Bowie T-shirt. If I were going to give Zack hell, I might as well read the whole catastrophe.

Sounds to me like you're going soft. Don't let the people out there sell you the Brooklyn Bridge, especially Lydia's old man—Frank Banning. They might throw a few rotten potatoes out to the poor and call it gleanings, but they'll line their pockets with the skin off your back. Look how Frank practically stole your grandmother's farm. If I'd had my wits about me, we would have found a land developer, and that ground would have put us all on easy street. I was young and green and let Banning take advantage of me, but you've been around, know the score. I've seen to that. So don't let them fill you full of that gleanings crap, kid.

<hr/>

49

Zack still doesn't know the score. He can't even tell the difference between my true love and some hoody kid off the street. Takes a lot of nerve for him to say I'm going soft. He'd be in jail or the poorhouse by now if he hadn't had me around to get him out of jams.

"Why are you crying, Pepper Junior?" Frankie handed me a bag of sugar.

"Frankie, you shouldn't sneak up on people like the Boston Strangler. You almost gave me a heart attack." I stuffed Zack's letter in my back pocket. I wasn't really in the mood to read any more of it anyway. "I'm not crying. I got a bug in my eye. It's the gnat season."

"Usually they come in August."

Frankie picked up some stones and bruised the breeze before he asked what I had been expecting.

"You get a letter from Rocky Rivers?"

"Two. And a wad of money from my dad. I guess Granny and I'll be sitting pretty until Zack and Miss Davis get married. Zack's got a new situation that's a sure thing, and he'll probably hate to leave such a good deal, but when I send him Miss Davis' picture, I bet he'll take the morning bus."

"Then I suppose Rocky Rivers will be coming too?"

"He's dying to, but I've been thinking maybe I'm too young to tie myself down. It'll probably break his heart, but I might write and tell him I'd like to play the field for a while."

"I think that's a real good idea. My sister Lydia

married Harvey Millbock when she was awfully young, and Dad says the whole family has been saddled with a shmuck longer than is natural. Harvey's a dentist." Frankie went back to the house smiling.

Granny and I had so much planning to do for the party, getting my costume together, making the taffy apples and everything, I just put Zack's letter out of my mind. When I read it to Granny, I improvised a little bit, and she was real pleased. I told her I imagined Zack would be coming home by spring, and that just tickled her pink. I didn't tell her my plan. Sometimes if you talk too much about an idea, the talking distracts you from doing it.

Our essays were due on Halloween. When I handed mine in after class I hung around to shoot the breeze with Miss Davis. In a campaign, you've got to play the odds. Frankie stayed too, but he's not much good for anything but moral support.

"Miss Davis, I just had a ball writing that paper, but my dad's such a fascinating man, it's hard to get him all down in five hundred words. I'd like to tell you some more about him, and since Frankie and I're throwing this party tonight, we wondered if you'd like to come. Didn't we Frankie?"

I had to grab his arm. He was heading for the door like a deserter.

"Sure. Unless you've got other plans, Miss Davis."

He said it like he hoped she did and never did raise

his eyes above the level of the garbage can. If we were going to get Miss Davis to be my mom, I was going to have to put Frankie through some training.

"How nice of you to ask me, Pepper. Unfortunately, I've made plans to go into the city this weekend to see a play."

"Isn't that a coincidence? My dad's just mad for the theater."

"But I'm interested in this party you and Frankie are having," Miss Davis went on before I could ask her who she was going with. "Since I won't be able to come, I wonder if you could manage another guest? I walked to school this morning with Chub Carruthers and he was telling me he hadn't made any plans for Halloween. I bet he would love to come to your party."

So Fallon hadn't invited Chub to her stupid party, and he had tattled to the teacher. What a creep. Frankie had his eyes pinned on me, like I was going to flash a neon sign across my forehead telling him to say no.

"Since Frankie and I are hosting it jointly, Miss Davis, I think we better have a conference. We'll be right back."

I pulled Frankie out in the hall and closed the door.

"Now I know you're thinking Chub will ruin our fun, Frankie, but we've got to be big about this. There're only two parties in town, right? Ours and Fallon's.

Now think how we would feel tonight if we didn't have anything to do on an important occasion like this."

"I know, Pepper Junior, but I was just thinking. We know our beach house is grand and everything, but I was just wondering if Chub would enjoy an outside party in October?"

"Chub's a blister. He'd complain if we were holding it at Buckingham Palace, but there's something else to consider. Since we've done all the work and the planning, he'd have to contribute something, right? We'll ask him to bring enough food so we can have supper. I've always liked giving dinner parties. They're more elegant, don't you think?"

Frankie still looked skeptical, but that's just his nature. The more I thought about sitting at the head of a dinner table with a gentleman on either side, candles flickering just like in that ad selling champagne I had cut out of a magazine, the better I liked it. Since we didn't have a lace tablecloth, I would see if Granny had any old curtains in the attic. I yanked Frankie back into the classroom before he could think of any more objections.

"Miss Davis, Frankie and I've talked it over, and Chub can come. But you tell him he has to wear a costume and bring food or it's no deal. His part is potato chips, Cokes, hot dogs, buns, and the trimmings. And tell him I like relish."

Five

Since Pepper arrived, things have really livened up, even at home. It seems like the Marlans are the most interesting topic my whole family has to discuss. Dad doesn't like my spending so much time with Pepper, but Mom says it's our Christian duty to look after the unfortunate. Dad told her the last time she made him do his Christian duty toward the Marlans he ended up paying twice what it was worth for a piece of ground that hadn't seen a speck of fertilizer for twenty years. She reminded him how much Granny's land had gone up in value now and said besides, it was better than having Zack Marlan in the family, which made my ears perk up, but that's all they said.

"Sometimes I wonder if having Harvey Millbock in

the family droning on about water drills and root canals has been much of an improvement," Dad said. "And to think I paid for a big piece of his learning about that crap."

"We needed a good dentist in the area," Mom said.

"Well, Lydia cost me a pretty penny that year," Dad said.

But I don't think Dad ever gets really mad at Lydia, no matter what she does. She's his firstborn and a lot like him everybody says. They also say she should have been the boy, and that makes me feel like I let everybody down. But my other three sisters all tell me it was worse being just another girl Dad didn't have any use for. I know he would cut my tongue out with his pocketknife if I said some of the things to him Lydia does. She's really pretty, a barrel of fun like Pepper, a terrific mother and everything, but Lydia is apt to be a little reckless and outspoken in public, and it always gets back to Dad.

Like when Lydia got her license suspended for speeding and it came out in the paper or the time she made a speech in the town hall favoring abortion, Dad liked to have had a fit, but she just tossed her head the way a horse that's wild will do and said since he had ruined her life when she was nineteen years old, what did he expect.

Right in front of Harvey and Dad, Lydia asked me what Pepper's dad was doing, but we were taking a walk on the beach by ourselves when she told me some details I hadn't known about.

"Mom thinks it's safe for you to hang around with Pepper Marlan because you're so young, but what she's never known is Zack and I started meeting in the barn when I was fourteen."

Seems to me like Lydia has always been way ahead of me when it comes to getting a job done. What I didn't tell her was how, even though I wasn't making out with Pepper in the barn yet, she had purified me. For weeks I hadn't had one of those dreams where I hypnotised Fallon O'Brien so I could have my way with her. Keeping up with Pepper takes so much energy, when my head touches that pillow, I just fall asleep.

Our Halloween party gave me some nightmares I could have done without though. Most of the time Chub Carruthers walks around as if a crab is biting his toe, and I couldn't see how he was going to add much to our fun. When Pepper gets excited about something, she moves around faster than the speed of light and expects everyone else to keep up. Now Chub's pace would have to speed up to be tedious, and I knew that was going to be a problem. But to tell the truth I was really worried about Pepper having her feelings hurt. I know she sees our beach house as being grand, and I just go right along with her when she talks about the veranda and the floor-to-ceiling picture window with a water view. But really it's just a few planks of driftwood we propped up and some rusty tin laid across the top for a roof. Chub Carruthers will never be able to see the veranda and the picture window, even on a dark night.

Pepper's talked herself into thinking he's just dying to come to our party, but I heard him tell Jeff Porter he was going to a big blast down in Riverhead that was being given by a sassy redhead with big breasts.

Mom and I had several disagreements about my costume. I didn't want to let Pepper down, but I would have felt like a fool in Dad's old army uniform. It was a mile too big. And I don't know how Mom could have expected me to act like a gypsy when I have never even seen one. Lydia finally saved the day when she bought an old derby hat at the swap shop and sewed some bright patches on a pair of Dad's baggy overalls. She painted a sad clown's face on me. I had the eyes for it, she said. The nearer it got to time to go the less I needed the makeup.

Pepper wanted us to come to the house first so Granny could see our getups. I might as well have been struck by lightning when I first saw Pepper's costume. She and Granny had raided the attic to find ruffled curtains for her skirt, but the blouse with rows and rows of yellowed lace had been one Mis' Marlan had worn when she was a girl. Granny had piled Pepper's hair up on top of her head in a doughnut arrangement, and since the punk paint was almost gone, she'd only sprayed a few curls around her face blue. Best of all was a cat-eyed half mask they'd concocted out of black dress material and a broken strand of pearls. Granny had glued it to her fly swatter handle, so Pepper could put it up to her face when she wanted to look flirtatious but she'd be able to get down to the beach without breaking her neck.

"Frankie, you look darling. Just like Emmett Kelly," Pepper said when she let me in. I've always noticed if you want women to start talking phony, all you have to do is let them get all gussied up. "Doesn't he look sweet, Granny?" She took a couple of twirls around the room so it was her ruffled curtains Granny and I were looking at rather than my derby hat.

"You look awful pretty, Pepper. Who're you supposed to be?"

"Merlina the Magician. Granny wanted me to be a bride and wear her wedding dress we found packed in tissue, but we decided to save it for a real wedding. It's gorgeous and hardly mildewed at all. About the size for Miss Davis, I'd imagine." Pepper winked at me like she did that first day in class.

When I heard the Carrutherses' car drive up, I began to sweat, but Pepper kind of glided to the door and puffed out her ruffles before letting in the biggest ghost I've ever set eyes on.

Chub was lugging two huge shopping bags under his sheet and having trouble.

"Here's the stuff you said I had to bring." He handed Pepper a bag with an enormous sack of potato chips on top. His sheet had holes cut for eyes, but he had to adjust it before he could find Granny. "Mis' Marlan, here's a leg of lamb from my dad's butcher shop."

"A leg off a lamb?" Pepper looked horrified. "Why we can't eat that."

"Oh, honey, lamb meat's the best there is," Granny said. She held up that hunk of flesh the way you do a newborn baby. "Favorite of mine for sure. But law, it's been so long, I can't remember when I've had me one to cook slow and juicy. Chub, you be sure to thank your folks for Pepper and me."

"In California we only eat the thighs, but shoot, I'll try anything once. Thanks, Chub, that was real nice of you."

"My mom made me bring it."

"Well listen, you guys, let's get this party on the road." Pepper was checking out the other shopping bag. "Granny, if you're sure you don't want to come down to the beach house with us, I'll just leave you a couple of these hot dogs, some potato chips, and a couple of buns so you can have a party right here in front of your fire." She broke open the buns, opened the mustard and catsup. "I might as well put some of

59

this stuff on for you, so you won't have to go looking for ours. Since I was having this dinner party, I didn't see any reason for Granny going to a lot of trouble for her supper," Pepper said to Chub, whose reaction to her dividing up his food was behind the sheet.

When we went down on the beach, we found a huge pile of wood Mis' Marlan had collected while we were at school. She'd set it in front of our beach house.

"Now, Frankie, you wait here with Chub, while I go create the right atmosphere."

Pepper lifted her ruffled skirt and ran. In a minute she had six jack-o'-lanterns blinking and the bonfire caught in a whoof. An old lace curtain was spread out on the veranda, and in the center she had filled a fish-bowl with colored beach glass.

"Now, Chub, you can come over to our beach house, but you must promise not to tell any of the other kids where it is, because this is our secret place."

"You think I'm crazy? I'm not going to tell anyone I came out here."

"Well then, Frankie and I won't tell there wasn't a blast in Riverhead or that the girl with the red hair and the big breasts was a figment of your warped imagination."

Pepper sat down Buddha fashion in front of the fish-bowl. "Before we eat and have the rest of the entertainment, I'll tell your fortunes."

The firelight cast moving shadows across Pepper's

face and if Chub would have shut up, I could have believed she was a fortune-teller. A real pretty one.

"Crap! You couldn't tell anyone's fortune. You're too wacky."

"The reason you have no faith in earthly things, Chub, is because you're destined to go to other planets as an astronaut. They're going to start making those capsules bigger any day now." She waved her hands over the bowl of glass, and closed her eyes. "I'm beginning to see a vision. There's a woman on the launching pad. Crying. She's begging you to come back to her. Your eyes are stony as they look up to the sky. She grabs your sleeve. 'Don't leave me, Chub, please . . .' You say, 'Unhand me, woman.' I think I recognize her. Ohmigod, it's Fallon O'Brien."

"No shit!"

"That's her, no doubt about it."

"Wouldn't she call me Charles, if I were an astronaut and all?"

"Probably Chuck. That sounds more like *The Right Stuff*."

"Pepper Junior, if it's all right with you, in my fortune I'd like to be called Franklin. Just to hear how it sounds."

Pepper threw her hands up so fast she liked to scared me and Chub both to death. "I think I've got it. I can almost hear it. Yes, they're saying, 'My fellow Americans, we're making this award today to Franklin

Banning for having discovered a new strain of potatoes that will stop hunger around the world. It's chock full of new vitamins.' I see you standing, walking toward the platform . . ."

"How tall am I?"

"Six, seven. There's a man on the front row wiping his eyes with a handkerchief. He's saying, 'That's my boy. That's my son Franklin, the best of the whole Banning tribe.' "

"Are there any girls?"

"One. A blonde. But I'm so hungry my vision's blurring. Let's fix dinner."

After we had roasted our weenies and eaten the taffy apples, Pepper started to wrap up what was left.

"I think I'll have another hot dog," Chub said.

"You've already had five. We're saving the rest for tomorrow."

"I brought them, and I won't be here tomorrow."

"You're a pig, you know that, Chub? How big do you think they're going to make those space capsules anyway? Now we're going to award prizes for the best costume, and then I'll choose a book from our library and give a reading. Frankie, you write our names in the sand. Then we'll all turn our backs while we take turns making a mark by the person's name who has the best costume. Frankie, you can count the votes. You won't cheat."

I found two marks for Pepper and one for Chub.

62

"Thank you for this honor," Pepper said. "The prize is that both of you get to kiss me."

I was mighty glad I had voted for Pepper instead of Chub. But I was afraid he was going to say something cruel to hurt Pepper's feelings. Instead he scrambled out from under that sheet like a flash and kissed her first. I had an urge to land my fist right in his lardy stomach. They kind of got mixed up though, and she turned her head a little bit just as he was zooming in. Chub's kiss landed on the corner, but mine found her mouth. Maybe I imagined it, but it felt like she sort of held on to it for a minute, like a suction cup. Probably she was just taking in a breath. She tasted like taffy.

"I know a ghost story, want to hear it?" Chub said.

"That'll add nice variety to our planned entertainment, Chub," Pepper said and sat down close to me.

"It's awful scary. I think you better sit between us, Pepper Junior, so we can protect you from the evil spirits." He moved over right next to her, so I scooted closer too till we were kind of like bookends for her. Chub's a pretty crummy storyteller, in my opinion. I didn't even think the story was very scary, but when Pepper went "ohhhh" and leaned against me, I put my arm around her and pretended to be scared too, so I could snuggle her up against me. I was even pretty sorry when the dumb story was over and Pepper jumped up and went into the beach house to get a book from the library I didn't even know we had. She came out with our only book wrapped in a plastic bag from the A&P. The book she had swiped!

"This book's been in our family for a long time. That's why I keep it wrapped up so it won't get damp. There's a story in here called "The Outcasts of Poker Flats" that Frankie and I like a lot, and since you are our guest tonight, Chub, I'll read it to you."

Pepper is a good storyteller. After a while my stomach even stopped churning with the fear Chub would notice Blueport Library stamped on the spine. When Mis' Marlan waved the lantern to let us know the Carrutherses had come to pick up Chub, we were both as quiet as the night. All you could hear were the waves slapping the beach and Pepper's voice reading:

And pulseless and cold, with a Derringer by his side and a bullet in his heart, though still calm as in life, beneath the snow lay he who was at once the strongest and yet the weakest of the outcasts of Poker Flats.

Six

Some people, like Jackie Kennedy and I, are just good at giving parties. Style's what we have, I guess. When we came back up to the house, Chub's older brother was tooting the horn, but Chub didn't seem to be in any hurry to leave.

"Mis' Marlan, my mom told me to be sure to tell you I had a nice time."

"We were glad to have you, son. Seems like old times having the house full of young folks again. My boy was well liked too."

"What're you guys going to do tomorrow? I guess I could come out if I had to. Since you kept my hot dogs, we probably better eat 'em pretty quick or they'll rot."

"Pepper and I always go to town on Saturday."

"But we're going to have a ton of parties. This was nothing compared to what I'm planning next. Probably it'll be black tie, you know like they have at the White House. I suppose your dad has turkeys in his butcher shop, and Frankie's mom can make hermits."

"I don't know why I always have to bring the most stuff. What're you contributing, Pepper Junior?"

"Class, Chub, a sense of class." I took Granny's old cardigan off the hook because there was a chill in the air, and I was thinking before long I'd be wearing ermine when I got all dressed up like this, the kind that doesn't scratch your neck. "I'll walk you partway home, Frankie, so we can start our plans. By the time we get to school on Monday, Chub, we'll have things all mapped out."

"I suppose I could meet you at Jake's tomorrow, since you'll have to know if I can get the turkey."

Frankie opened the door and ushered us out to the backyard. "Pepper and I aren't going to Jake's tomorrow. We have lots of errands to do, and . . . and we might have to babysit for Lydia's kids."

"Too bad ole Trenton got sent to reform school or he could take care of his little sisters."

"I'll bust you in the mouth, Chub Carruthers, if you don't stop lying like that. Trenton's in military school and you know it."

Chub's brother opened the window and said, "Fat-

ass, if you don't get in this car, you can walk to Blueport."

"He's the one that should've gone to reform school."
Frankie nodded toward the car.

"But Trenton's the one who got caught, right? And
he thought he was such a hotshot."

"So did your sister."

I think we might have had a rumble right in our
backyard, if Chub's brother hadn't started to drive off
without him, and he had to run, well, as much as Chub
can, to get in.

"Who's Trenton and what does he have to do with
Chub's sister?"

Frankie started walking down the road faster than
his usual pace. I guess he was still aching to punch
Chub out.

"Trenton is my sister Lydia's oldest son. He's quite
a bit older than me. She had him the first year Harvey
was in dental school. Said she wasn't ready for a kid
like Trenton. But even though he's always getting in
bad, I think Lydia likes him best. It's funny, but then
he's real good-looking and has a way with women.
Chub's sister was nuts about him."

"Why'd he get sent away?"

"Harvey thought it'd be best for him. I think he was
running with a fast crowd, getting into a lot of scrapes.
We don't talk about it much at home. But Trenton

really livened things up. I miss him. So does Lydia."

"Like my dad misses me, I guess, but I just had to come out here to take care of Granny." I climbed up on the rail fence bordering the road. The moon was full, and the white light softened things. "I hope Rocky Rivers doesn't do anything desperate, like drink poison Kool-Aid, when he finds out I'll have to stay here. Since Dad's going to marry Miss Davis, and Granny's so old, I really don't have any choice. And this place's not bad. You know, until we grow up."

"Then where do you want to live?"

"The White House, I think. I don't suppose you'd be interested in being president?"

"Oh, I don't think I could handle that, Pepper Junior. Making all those speeches on television. Giving book reports gives me a stomachache."

"I suppose the country will be ready for a woman president by the time we're old enough. I don't think I'd be afraid of the TV cameras, and I always did want to take a ride in a helicopter."

"If you're going to be president, what can I be?"

"We could dress you in drag, and you could be first lady!" I almost fell off the fence laughing. Frankie pouring tea in a pink suit and high heels really tickled my funny bone.

"Almost as funny as a woman with blue hair in the Oval Office."

"Maybe we'll have to promise not to get married,

like the nuns and the priests. Then I'll make you my Secretary of Agriculture."

"Why can't I get married?"

"If you think I'm going to have someone like Fallon O'Brien smiling at all the men at the parties I give, you're nuts."

"Nancy Reagan does."

"That's what I mean. Fallon would bat her eyes at the guy with a finger on the red button, as long as he wore pants. We've got to take our responsibilities seriously, Frankie, save the world. First thing I'd do is take all those bombs to Mars and leave them there."

"You'll probably make a good president, Pepper Junior."

"I think so."

"If I don't get on home, my dad's going to skin me, even if I am hanging out with the future president. See you tomorrow."

Monday in English class I was still thinking about being president when a better opportunity turned up.

"The freshman class has been asked to put on a one-act play for the November assembly," Miss Davis said. "By borrowing rather substantially from a skit my sorority did in college, I've put together a play called *Elizabeth and Essex*. All of you will have an opportunity to be involved with the production."

Production, fiddle. I was going to be Queen Elizabeth! My perfect role. An opportunity for this crummy school to finally see my real talent.

"Billy, you'll be in charge of sets. Pick a crew to work with you. Melinda Sue, you'll do costumes, and Chub, you will be casting director."

I could see what Miss Davis was doing. She assigned kids no one would pick to collect the garbage to tasks, so they'd have something to do. Her making Chub the guy to choose the cast was a stroke of luck for me. I told Frankie inviting Chub to our party would pay off. I was so excited my heart was beating a tattoo on my rib cage.

Chub sat in the last seat in the next row of desks. I turned around and said to him, "My Halloween costume will work just grand. All I'll need is a crown." I jumped out of my seat and started striding back toward his seat. I spraddled my legs and walked like a duck with a heavy stride just like I'd seen Elizabeth I do on TV. "This is how I'll play her."

Fallon covered her face and didn't make a sound, but as soon as she did, the room sounded like a laugh track for NBC. I just hate it when people show their ignorance and laugh at you like a herd of donkeys, but you just have to think about something else and not let them hurt your feelings. I went back to my seat and concentrated on how I'd get Granny in to see the show. Maybe Mrs. Banning would bring her. I looked at Frankie, but he had laid his head down on his desk like he might be sick.

When those dummies stopped hehawing, Miss Davis' face was flushed, and she looked at me as if she didn't feel well either.

"Pepper Junior, I thought you might like to do the makeup. I bet you would be good at it."

"Thank you, Miss Davis, but I'd be better as Queen Elizabeth."

"Chub gets to pick who's the queen, doesn't he, Miss Davis?" That fink Alice Parker surely didn't think she'd get the part.

"Yeah, Chub gets to pick," Jeff Porter yelled.

Everybody turned around to look at Chub who had seemed shocked at first, but when he began to get everyone's attention he started acting real cocky. He kind of pushed out his lip and bounced around in his seat like he was Cecil B. deMille.

"I haven't made my decision yet," he said, in a real haughty tone, I thought. "When I'm good and ready I'll let you know."

I don't think things were going as Miss Davis had planned. She was fussing around with some papers on her desk and she kept looking at the clock like she wished it would move faster.

"Why don't we let Chub have a chance to read the script and he can announce his cast tomorrow. In the meantime I would like to pass back the papers you wrote about an unforgettable character. I've written comments. Some of you did an excellent job of making your subjects seem real."

I was wondering if it were possible to fall in love with someone you just read about on a piece of paper and half wishing I'd asked Frankie's mom to pray for Miss Davis to go bonkers over Zack. As often as she goes to church, she probably runs out of things to ask the Lord. Miss Davis used a green pen to mark our papers. She wasn't the type to hand them back dripping in the blood of red ink like some of those nerds I had to put up with in California. She had written on mine:

Pepper, you show a natural flair for writing. Your flamboyant style holds your reader's attention and creates an interest in your subject. You also are aware of your reader and very persuasive when it comes to influencing him/her to be sympathetic to your subject. [Sympathetic? What did she mean? Zack would punch anyone who made the mistake of feeling sorry for him.] However, I could not determine if you were using hyperbole for comic effect, or if your enthusiasm for your topic led you to extravagant exaggeration. [Exaggeration? When she marries Zack, she'll be sorry she wrote that on my paper.] For example, it would have been more effective to have used only one simile per sentence—"My dad is handsomer (more handsome) than David Bowie, has more karisma (sp) than the Kennedies, has Onassis' ability to make money when the right opportunity turns up, and that's why even women like Sally Ride chase after him all the time even though he's waiting for the right woman to turn him on—someone solid and nice who won't run around on him, like maybe a teacher," makes too many comparisons in one sentence. A good writer is able to explain complicated things very simply. B –

Well, like she said, I'd gotten her interest. After she sees me playing Queen Elizabeth, she'll be dying to have a daughter with so much talent.

The bell rang, but I'd been so wrapped up in Miss Davis' comments I didn't have my things together, so I was still in my seat when Chub and Fallon walked past.

"Oh, Chub, I think you'd look cute in an astronaut suit," Fallon was saying. "Why I'd be scared to death to let them shoot me clear off the earth in a burst of fire. You're really brave."

The way he was mooning after her, I could tell he'd already forgotten all about Halloween.

When we ran out to get on the bus at the end of the day, the weather had changed. A cold wind had blown up and the temperature must have dropped fifteen or twenty degrees. I had goose pimples. The cold air cut through my Levi jacket before I could get on the heated bus. Granny's going to look through her rag bag to see if she can find one of her mens' flannel shirts to make a real sharp lining for my jacket like the cowboys wear. I was thinking it was time for us to get busy on our project when Frankie scooted into the seat next to me and gave me an inside chill.

"Temperature dropped below freezing finally," he said. "At least now I won't have to spend any more time picking cabbage and cauliflower."

"Why not? There's still a lot of them in the field back of your house. Are they gleanings?"

"Truck farming's over after the first frost. Vegetables are no good after they freeze. Even the gleaners wouldn't want them."

"Ohmigod! I don't think we've got all of ours in. Frankie, you've got to help me. Granny's too old to be bending and stooping in that garden. We've still got some real nice tomatoes good enough for soup. In California, people eat frozen vegetables all the time."

"Well, I never thought of it that way."

"While we're picking, I'll tell you how I'm going to play Queen Elizabeth."

"I wish you wouldn't get your heart set on being in that play, Pepper Junior. I've noticed things don't very often work out the way we hope they will."

"This time they will. I'm a natural for the part, and

Chub owes me for asking him to our party. If you want to be Essex, I'll tell him he has to cast you. Then after we give it at school, we could keep on giving it in our beach house. We could invite all the neighbors and serve refreshments."

"I don't want to be Essex! Mom made me be a Wise Man in a church play when I was ten, and I forgot my lines. Couldn't remember a word even with Essie Robinson hissing them at me from the choir loft. Mortified myself and the whole family."

"Well, you'll just play Essex at home then. You won't freeze up if I'm the only one there."

"Listen, Pepper, why don't we just work on the play we're going to give? Forget all about that old school play. Who wants to prance around in front of those kids anyway?"

"I do."

Frankie and I collected a bushel of almost perfect vegetables we had overlooked in our garden. Anything that was going a little soft, Granny and I just plopped in the soup pot. They soften right up anyway. After he went home, I told Granny I was going to the beach house, but I took the boat and rowed out to Bob Gillespie's lobster traps. He picks up in the morning, and he'd already caught four more lobsters. I took two of those old pinchers. Bob's real friendly. Waves at us every morning when he's out there hauling. I knew he would have dropped us off a couple if he had thought about it and knew how much Granny does love a lobster steamed in saltwater and seaweed. As soon as I get the money together, I'm going to get us a license like Grandpa had when he was alive. Then we'll invite the Gillespies over for supper and pay them back for these two they won't even miss. I told Granny a trap had washed up on the shore without a buoy, just so she wouldn't be worried about owing Bob Gillespie until I could get our license.

I went to bed that night full of lobster and dreams of playing Queen Elizabeth. I fell asleep wondering if they'd make me dye my hair red like the TV actress.

The next morning in English class, I could hardly wait for Miss Davis to finish taking attendance. After she closed the book, she said, "Chub, I've written the characters on the board. Why don't you fill in the names you've chosen to play the parts."

Jeff Porter moved his chair just far enough out into the aisle so Chub had to turn sideways to get through and then he made a sound like a pig, so everybody started to laugh, of course. Chub put his arm across his jelly-roll stomach and bowed about a dozen times. He's the kind of kid who would rather be ridiculed than ignored. I just wished he'd get on with it and write my name up there. My heart wasn't beating regular and with the windows all closed tight, there didn't seem to be enough air for all of us. Frankie must have been feeling it too because he had his head on his desk again.

Miss Davis had written the list according to their importance in the play, but to drag out getting some attention for a change, Chub started at the bottom and wrote in slow motion. Just to show how much Chub knows about casting, he gave the part of Essex to that stupid Jeff Porter who would probably try to spoil my performance.

Since Elizabeth was the star, the room got quiet when Chub put the chalk on the board next to her name. Zack took me to the track in Santa Ana once, and when the horses came into the stretch, the stands got quiet just like that. I leaned forward in my seat trying to will him to write a P on that board. He turned around and looked at me with a big grin on his face, but it kind of melted away for a minute. He jerked his head real quick and looked at Fallon. She gave him that same Cheshire cat smile she reserves for no one. What a flirt! Even when he made the first stroke and drew a straight line, I still thought he might connect a curved line to it. But when you put your hopes on a hog like Chub, it never works out. He gave the part to Fallon.

Everybody started to clap and Melinda Sue, who'd sell her mother for a chance to run around with Fallon, started chanting, "Speech! The star should make a speech."

"I'd like to thank Chub and everyone for giving me this wonderful part, but I just feel awful because I know how much Pepper Junior wanted it."

Working outside in the cold last night must have given me an awful cold, and it made me so mad because I didn't have a handkerchief. I jumped up.

"That's all right, Fallon. I'm coming down with pneumonia and won't be able to play the role anyway." I wiped my nose on my sleeve. "I have to go to the nurse," I said to Miss Davis. "Besides, I didn't want to be in the damned old play anyway." I slammed the door the way Spike does and hoped he heard it way down in the principal's office. I hoped he'd expel me until I was sixteen when I could quit without going to jail.

I was sitting on a wooden keg behind the furnace figuring how long it would take me to hitch to Oakland when Henry our janitor, who has become a friend of mine, came down there.

"Whata you crying for, Pepper Junior?"

"I'm not crying. I've got this allergy that acts up unless I have a cigarette every day. It's a rare strain that only nicotine can control. You got one?"

Henry reached in his coverall pocket and handed me a cigarette. "If Spike catches you, you know I'll have to say you stole it?"

"Sure."

"Maybe you shouldn't have tried to come back here.

You can't help if your daddy got mixed up with those gambling fellers over in the Hamptons, and Mis' Marlan had to sell her land to pay them off. But folks around here don't forget things like that."

"He was just a kid. How was he supposed to know about thugs like them? Granny doesn't blame him a bit."

"I know. Folks always said she spoiled him, him coming along so late in her life, her old man dying so soon and all. But I liked Zack myself. Good-looking boy. Pleasant young feller to be around. The first year I was stoking this furnace, he and Lydia Banning used to sneak down here to fool around. I never told nobody on 'em."

Henry tapped a gauge with his finger and then lit up himself. I was wondering how much liquid fat Chub would make if I stuffed him in the furnace.

"I was right surprised when Lydia up and married Harvey Millbock so soon after Zack left. She and Zack used to be real sweet on each other."

"What could she do, after Zack had sense enough to blow this burg? I'm thinking about moving on myself. Thought I might head out for Hollywood tomorrow. Try my luck at the movies, you know?"

"With some fancy clothes, you could be right pretty, Pepper. But the way I hear it, getting a part can be awful hard."

"At least in Hollywood you'd be dealing with professionals who knew what they were doing. Not like the amateurs you have to put up with in this stupid school. Around here Greta Garbo's talent could have gone unnoticed."

"Somebody up there hurt your feelings?" He nodded toward the ceiling that sounded as if it was going to cave in. Classes were changing, but if they thought I was going to go pay court to her majesty Fallon O'Brien, or sit in a history class with that traitor Chub Carruthers, they were nuts.

"Nobody can hurt your feelings unless you let them, and I don't care a twit about Fallon O'Brien or Chub Carruthers. When I get to be a famous Hollywood actress, I'll probably zip right past them both in my limousine and not even speak."

"That Chub does seem like his daddy stuffed him too full of his good baloney, but that little O'Brien girl seems like a sweet child."

"That's all you know!"

"Pepper? Are you down here, Pepper?"

"Sounds like you've at least got one friend. Ain't that Frankie Banning's voice?"

I didn't feel like facing Frankie, to tell the truth. Since I was probably coming down with a cold or TB or something. But Henry stretched and said he'd better be getting after those wastebaskets in the cafeteria. He walked right around to where Frankie was standing.

"Henry, have you seen Pepper Marlan?"

Henry motioned him toward the furnace, and went out saying, "Seems like history just keeps repeating itself around this school."

"What did he say?" Frankie asked.

"He's just muttering to himself."

I turned my back and looked out the little basement window like I saw something interesting in the parking lot. The germs crawling around in me were probably making my eyes all red and puffy. No use advertising when you don't look your best.

Frankie put his arm around my shoulders and that just made my cold worse. He laid his head up against mine and then my lungs began to hurt too, and I started to sob. I just couldn't stop it.

"I'm sorry you didn't get the part. I think you'd have been a real pretty Queen Elizabeth. And you're spunky like she was, too."

He turned around and I hid my face in his shoulder. For a while he just held me. Then he bent his head down and I raised up and he kissed me. His lips were so soft and felt so good. When I was beginning to need to breathe, I opened my mouth a little bit, and he did too. I began to feel warm all over and just plain forgot about breathing at all.

"I love you, Pepper Junior," he whispered in my ear.

"I thought you loved Fallon O'Brien."

"Not anymore. Since you came, I hardly think about her at all. But I suppose you're still in love with Rocky Rivers?"

"You know it's the funniest thing. I can't hardly even remember what he looks like."

Seven

Mom thought something was wrong with me because I got ready to go to church with her on Wednesday night without her even pestering me. I don't know if it does any good or not, but the preacher always says he will pray for my soul, and I was feeling as if I needed the help.

Seems like my head is always itching recently with ideas that have no business being there. I never wanted to smash anyone in the mouth until the night of our Halloween party, and that's all I wanted to do to Chub Carruthers the whole evening. All weekend I felt bad about having turned violent, until Monday in English class when I wished I had killed him.

Having wicked thoughts about Chub Carruthers is

one thing, but when I started wishing bad things would happen to Fallon O'Brien, I knew the preacher had a job on his hands saving my soul. Two months ago I was planning on marrying Fallon, and now here I was hoping she would have a bad accident so she couldn't show off as Queen Elizabeth. Fallon has not changed a bit. I'm the one who has turned mean.

But I've been meaning to have Mom ask the preacher why there is so much unfairness in the world. Fallon has everything going for her. Pretty as a movie star. Guys all loony over her. She has a real warm green coat and plenty to eat. Makes the kind of grades my folks dream about. Since it has turned cold, I've been thinking the good Lord did not give Pepper her fair share of anything.

The look on her face when she didn't get to be the star hurt my heart. Even though no one was about to admit it, after she ran out of class crying, I don't think those other kids thought it was so funny anymore either. Miss Davis made a strange sound in her throat, the way you do when you're trying to catch your breath, and she didn't say another word about the lousy play. She told us to read chapter ten of *Great Expectations*. I guess she forgot we already read that chapter, and no one reminded her. I think everybody was glad to have the chance to hide their faces behind their books. Our class never has been so quiet.

When the bell finally rang, I took a chance on getting killed for being late to history and went looking for Pepper. I thought she would probably be hanging out with Henry in the boiler room. Spike says anyone who doesn't play by the rules puts a hole in the school's defensive line, but Henry is not much of a team player. He is awful good to the kids, though, especially Pepper.

I went down there to try and cheer her up. I thought I would get her talking about rock stars in California or stopping nuclear war. Something distracting. But I was the one who got distracted.

Before, Pepper had always seemed bigger than real to me, but there she was having to stand on her tiptoes to see out of the basement window. Wounded, she looked so little, I had this crazy idea if I didn't hold on to her she would limp off into the tall grass and die alone. Just imagining not having Pepper around made me feel more miserable than I did when a truck hit Blackie or my grandfather died.

When I took hold of her, I was just thinking about keeping her from disappearing, but you can't imagine how wonderful she felt. I used to worry a lot about how you went about putting your arms around a girl and getting her in the right spot to kiss her. Guys in the movies never have any trouble, but they get to practice. I was always afraid I would be awkward, but that's one thing I seemed to have been born knowing how to do, and I can't even show my dad. Pepper fit up against me perfect.

One thing holding a girl and kissing her makes a guy do is feel his responsibility. When you find out how soft they are, you know they could never protect themselves against much of anything. And Pepper was crying.

Like I said I really just went down there to try to make her cheerful, but then I started kissing her, and it was like I never wanted to stop. I didn't want to stop because it felt so good, but also I was afraid we would feel silly and not know what to say. I mean after a girl has put the tip of her tongue in your mouth, and you've told her how much you love her, you can't just say we better go to history or we're going to get detention.

First I heard Henry whistling. I didn't even know he could. Pepper and I jumped about a mile apart.

"Spike's coming," Henry said and then went to rearranging the brooms he had hanging on the wall.

Pepper sat down on a wooden keg and clutched her stomach. I thought she was dying. I've never seen such a pitiful expression on anyone's face.

"Ooooh. Frankie, I want to thank you for coming down here with me and saving my life." She was talking awful loud and funny. "I think I've split my gall bladder. You better go call your mom to come get us."

"I caught you red-handed this time."

You just don't realize how big Spike is till he's towering over you, rubbing his hands like he's getting in shape to pull your arm off.

"Oh, Mr. Spade, we're so glad to see you. You've really come to our rescue." Pepper reached out a hand to him, but then she must have had another pain because she doubled up. "Oooooh. I got so sick in class, and Frankie was kind enough to bring me down here where I could get some air. And I've taken worse. He was afraid to leave me, even to go get you."

"Now, Pepper, you cut it out. I know you're faking." Spike wrinkled his nose and sniffed. "And I think I smell smoke."

"One of my friends out in California got sick at school, and they thought she was faking. She died!" Pepper started studying the ceiling. "Her folks really missed her, but they're feeling better since they sued the principal for a million dollars."

"But you're not even sick."

"It's inside." Pepper punched her stomach. "My granny wouldn't want to make any trouble for anyone, but I don't know about my dad."

I felt like I was watching a tennis match, and if Pepper dropped the ball, it was going to be the end of both of us.

"I went to school with your dad." Spike was thinking hard, and Pepper didn't interrupt him.

"Frankie, you see that she gets to the nurse's office,

87

and then, young man, you better get yourself to class."

I grabbed Pepper's arm before she could say anything else.

"Okay, Mr. Spade."

After he had stomped out of sight, I said, "Pepper, does your gall bladder really hurt?"

"Of course not."

"Well, what're you going to tell the nurse?"

"I'll take a nap on her couch and then tell her I was probably just getting my period."

When Pepper says things you're not prepared for like that, it makes my neck itch. There's just no way a guy can keep his composure hanging around with a girl like Pepper whose moods change faster than the weather in winter. She doesn't need a stage to be a star performer. At least her last scene with Spike had made me forget about feeling awkward because I had kissed her.

Lydia and Harvey and the kids came for supper that night, but Mom made me go up to do my homework after dessert. My room's on the corner in the back and has so many windows sometimes the moonlight keeps me awake. White light, Pepper calls it. I didn't really feel like drawing the parts of the heart or writing a report on the gross natural products of Argentina, so I looked out the window up toward Pepper's house, just to see if her light showed through the trees. She was coming down the road with a sack slung over the back of her Levi jacket. I couldn't imagine what she was doing out after dark with the wind whipping up like it was. She had her shoulders scrunched up like she was cold, but her hair was blowing like one of those models on TV.

I was thinking about sneaking down the back stairs and going out there and giving her a hug, just to keep her warm, when she stopped at the end of the field. I jumped back in the shadows when she looked up toward the house, as if she were checking it out. Then she began to fill her sack with potatoes from our gleanings pile, looking up toward the house every time she put one in. When Spot barked at something, she fell flat on the ground behind the pile and lay still until he stopped his yapping. I ran into the bathroom across the hall and closed the door. I stayed in there for a long time with my face hidden in Dad's robe hanging behind the door. I felt awful, like a peeping Tom. Like I had betrayed Pepper.

I was hoping Granny and Pepper weren't going to get sick from eating all of those frozen vegetables when I heard Lydia at the bottom of the steps.

"Frankie, have you finished your homework? Can I come up?"

I came out of the bathroom and sat on the top step. I wanted to head her off from going into my room, just in case Pepper was still out there.

"Sure, Lyd. Come on up. Sit down."

She was wearing a pale gray turtleneck sweater. "Pretty," I said. It was so soft it felt as if it were melting on my fingers.

"Thanks. This sweater always reminds me of Trenton's eyes."

"I bet you've got lots of clothes stuffed away in your closet, Lydia. Things you wouldn't even miss. Like warm jackets and sweaters and stuff."

She tilted her head and looked at me funny till I felt like squirming. "What're you up to, honey? You want me to give somebody clothes?"

"No. Not give them to her, exactly."

"What've you got in mind?"

"I was thinking maybe you could tell her you were donating them to the Swap Shop. Maybe make her believe you didn't even remember what they looked like. She wouldn't like to think anybody knew she was wearing hand-me-downs, so we'd have to fix it so she could take them without you knowing. . . ."

"Pepper?"

"Yeah."

"Now, Frankie, let me see if I've got this straight. You want me to arrange it so Pepper can steal some clothes from me, right? And when I see her wearing them, I'm not supposed to recognize they're mine?"

"Kind of like that. Not stealing exactly. But making it easy for her to take them without hurting her pride. You understand?"

"Sure." She rumpled my hair and put an arm around my shoulder. "You're the best of the lot, you know that, Frankie. No matter what Dad says."

"Lydia, I don't suppose you have a red jacket lying around, do you? I think Pepper would look beautiful in a bright red jacket."

"I'll see." She put her chin in her hands and looked kind of dreamy. Sad like. "Zack's not sending her any money?"

"He's going to when they find the mother lode in this gold mine he invested in."

My sister's moods swing as wildly as Pepper's. She laughed and laughed. "A gold mine? Oh, that's wonderful!"

Mom appeared at the bottom of the stairs, and when she saw us, she came up and sat with us on the steps.

"Frankie was just telling me about the gold mine Zack Marlan's about to get a piece of. See? I tried to tell you and Dad you were wrong about Zack's prospects."

Lydia was grinning, but Mom looked as if her tooth hurt.

"Lydia, Lydia. You romanticized that boy all out of proportion. Don't tell me you're still doing it—after all this time? You, married to a respectable, professional man like Harvey? Three beautiful children?"

"Especially Trenton. Don't you think he is especially beautiful, Mom?"

Mom darted a quick look at me, but I ducked my head. When Lydia gets in one of her feisty moods, you never know what's going to happen in our family.

"God tells us in Genesis, 'In pain shall thou bring forth children.' You make me conscious of it almost every day, Lydia. Not that I don't love you, but your father and I did what we thought was best for you, and all we've ever gotten for it is abuse."

"I just get so bored. Zack never bored me."

"When he decided to leave here, Lydia, you know he was involved with another girl over on the South Fork."

"Decided to leave? Now that's rich. I thought Dad bought him off and ran him out of the state. And he wasn't *involved* with Cathy Blake. We'd just had a spat and he was trying to make me jealous."

"That wasn't just a spat he was having with those gamblers. Zack told Dad himself they'd kill him if he didn't pay them what he owed."

"He would never have started gambling if Dad hadn't made him feel as if he had to have a pot of gold before we could get married."

Usually, Mom made me leave the room when this subject came up. I wondered if she finally thought I had grown up or if she had just forgotten I was there.

"I'm glad you didn't marry Zack Marlan, Lydia. If you had, I'd have been Pepper's uncle."

I should have kept my mouth shut. Lydia hugged

me, but Mom said, "Frankie, I'm going to check that homework before you go to sleep, so if it's not done, you better get at it."

Pepper should have been home by then, so reluctantly, I went to my room. "Lydia, you won't forget?" I said before I closed the door. She gave me a thumbs-up sign and winked.

Mom came in before she went to bed. I had to tell her what my heart was supposed to be, but after I explained it to her, she said it would probably be okay since I had labeled the parts and she doubted my science teacher had ever seen a real one. She tried to make me tell her what Lydia and I were cooking up, but I couldn't.

"I don't know what's to become of your sister, Frankie, I really don't. Nineteen years she's been married, and she's still flighty. Tomorrow she's driving all the way into Manhattan to shop. She announced that downstairs just before they left. When Harvey asked her why she wanted to do that when his mother always came to dinner on Tuesdays, she says, 'a whim.' Then she wrinkles her nose at him and says, 'Let's be daring and have your mother on Wednesday.' Harvey lets her get away with it too." Mom rubbed her waist the way she's always doing. Lydia says she wears her girdle too tight. "If I behaved that way, your father'd have me put in the loony farm," she said as she was leaving.

I wondered if Dad wouldn't kind of like it if Mom

did something crazy now and then. Lydia did silly things all the time, and she was his favorite. One Friday night when I stopped at The Quiet Man with him and Mr. Terry, I saw Dad pinch Ruby Clark's behind, and Mom's always said Ruby was the biggest fool in town.

Pepper's like Lydia. She just doesn't let things get her down for long. She was only mopey for a couple of days after Fallon got to be Queen Elizabeth, and then she got this idea for us to make stained glass windows. Since it was too cold to be outside, Granny spread newspapers on her table and we worked there. That worried me because it was pine and looked like one my sister Ruth had paid an arm and a leg for at Julie's Antiques.

"Mis' Marlan, isn't this an antique?" I asked while Pepper was spreading out the beach glass according to color. "We might get glue on it."

"No, Frankie, it's just old like me. You can't hurt it."

To tell the truth, I was worried about the glue too. It looked just like the kind we used in art class at school.

"Frankie, we'll practice sticking pieces on this driftwood. Then when we get the hang of it, we'll start doing windows for churches. Maybe for advertising purposes we'll donate one to your mom's church. It could stand some jazzing up. When we've made a mint of money, I think I'll take Granny around the world on one of those big ships. You too, of course."

"Now won't we have ourselves a time," Granny said. She stroked Pepper's hair as she passed by to stir the soup simmering on the stove.

Mis' Marlan was an awful fine lady, but I wished she wasn't going to be with us. I hadn't had a chance to kiss Pepper again since that day in the boiler room, and I was afraid it would be just the same way on the ship.

I was thinking maybe Saturday when we went to town, if there was nobody in the stacks at the library, that might be a good place. But then Thursday night Lydia called and said she had the clothes ready. I was so worried I even forgot about kissing Pepper. I just don't have any talent for lying.

"What did Lydia want?" Mom asked when I got off the phone.

"Uh, she wants Pepper and me to take some old clothes to the Swap Shop for her Saturday."

"That girl better not be giving any of her clothes away. You heard what happened to her in Manhattan Tuesday?"

"No."

"I stopped in to have Harvey clean my teeth today, and he told me. You can bet Lydia never would. She went wild shopping at Saks Fifth Avenue when she was in the city. Spent four hundred dollars, and everything was stolen out of the car before she even got home."

"No kidding!"

"Like Harvey said, here they'll get a Saks bill for four hundred dollars this month, and not a thing to show for it. Lydia's just careless. Always has been."

Saturday I didn't think Lydia was careless at all. She helped me work out all the details.

When we got to town, just like Lydia and I had planned, I said to Pepper, "I have to get a haircut, but Lydia wanted us to take some clothes to the Swap Shop for her, and I wondered if you'd do it while I have my ears lowered. They're just some old things she had in the back of the closet and forgot what they looked like. Why I bet if Lydia met someone walking down the street with them on, she wouldn't even recognize them. She's got so many clothes, she can't even remember what she has, I swear she can't. Lydia's flighty, Mom says. Probably affects her memory."

"Okay, I've got it," Pepper said. I knew I was going on too much, but I couldn't make myself shut up. "Where do I find them?"

"She left them in a duffle bag in the living room. Door's open, but she and the girls aren't home. Anyone who wanted to could just walk right in there and try those clothes on. You just take your time, Pepper. Don't hurry on my account. Sometimes it takes Harry hours to cut my hair. And Lydia's not going to be home for a long time. Like maybe midnight."

When I finally got in that barber's chair, I collapsed. I was exhausted.

Unfortunately Harry zipped right through my haircut, and I had to hang around reading *Time* magazine while I watched for Pepper. Dad says the poor president really has his hands full fighting those Communists that seem to be sprouting up everywhere like ragweed. Just from looking at the pictures in *Time*, I couldn't figure out how the man kept it all straight. Grenada and Central America were bad enough, but the corker was that Mid-East business. My history teacher would probably flunk me if he knew, but I can never tell exactly whose side it is we're supposed to be on. But since I got myself involved in this scheme to get Pepper some clothes, at least I've got a better feeling for just how hard strategic planning can be.

When I finally saw her sauntering down the street with Harvey's duffle bag slung over her back, I felt as if I'd just managed to pull off D-Day.

"That Swap Shop's an interesting place," Pepper said. "After I dropped off your sister's clothes, I gave them a few bucks and picked up some rags for Granny to use in her rugs. Let's leave these in your mother's car and then see what's happening over at Jake's."

I was such a basket case, I stepped on her toe when I tried to take the duffle bag off her back so I could put it in the car. She breathed right in my face. Cripes! She'd been drinking!

Eight

As impractical as Zack can be, we can all count our blessings that he and Lydia Banning didn't team up. Frankie thinks she's flighty, but that woman's really nuts.

Since I had some time to kill while Frankie got his haircut, I checked out those clothes she was throwing out, and you would not believe what I found. The gray flannel slacks fit me like they'd been tailored, and the turtleneck sweater that matched was soft as sugar and didn't have a spot or any sign of wear at all. But the red pea coat was what really freaked me out. When I slipped my arm in the sleeve, my fingers hit a ticket that showed that crazy woman had never even had that jacket on. Saks Fifth Avenue must have been ashamed to clip that outrageous $150 price tag on the outside.

I always knew I had outstanding taste. That jacket was the very one I would have picked off a rack, even before I saw it cost as much as a mink.

Lydia had a big mirror in a gold frame in her dining room, so I did a couple of turns in front of it, getting the full effect of my good fortune. If those *Vogue* photographers could see me in that outfit, Brooke Shields would have to go into retirement.

She had left her gray wool gloves in the pocket and was throwing out a matching scarf that must have been three yards long. I could wrap it around my ears and throw the ends over my shoulder in a way that added a lot of dash. I could hear an announcer saying, "Coming down the runway now, ladies and gentlemen, Miss Pepper Junior Marlan in what the well-dressed young woman of today is just dying to own." I strutted down that runway and it led me right into Lydia's kitchen. Modeling is hard work, eats up a lot of calories, so I thought I might as well check out her refrigerator to see if I could find a snack to give me some energy before I tried on the rest of the stuff. She had some ham and just dozens of cans of beer. Since I knew she'd want to find a way to thank me for taking these things off her hands and giving her some room in her closet, I fixed a sandwich and opened a can of Bud. It was kind of bitter, but I was so thrilled with the other things Lydia had put in that duffle bag, I hardly knew what I was tasting anyway.

Seems like my granny is one of those women who has spent her whole life figuring out what she can do for other people and never did get around to doing much for herself. So, knowing how much it would please her, when I went home, I told her Zack had sent me the new clothes. I also invented a letter where he said the blue cardigan was for her. She spent half the afternoon hugging that sweater to her breast and telling me what a fine boy he was. I scooted her rocker closer to the fire, so I had some space to put on a fashion show for her. We had a ball deciding how different combinations could make me a whole slew of outfits. I was going to be the best-dressed girl at Port of Egypt High School, no doubt about that. Fallon O'Brien was going to eat her heart out when she saw my red pea coat.

You never can tell who might decide to break into those school lockers, so I wore my jacket to classes rather than take the chance of having it stolen. No one could take their eyes off it. Having people stare at you is just the price you pay for being well dressed. Frankie was the only one who actually said how pretty I looked, but I could tell everyone else thought so too.

Frankie and I had hardly gotten in the door for English class when Miss Davis said, "What a beautiful jacket, Pepper Junior."

"Thank you, Miss Davis, my dad sent it to me. He has awful good taste, and likes for his women to look sharp. If he were married to a nice woman, he'd probably want to cover her in silk and diamonds."

I was going to tell her about the other things he had sent and how generous he could be, but Frankie practically jerked my arm off, and said, "We better sit down, Pepper Junior. It's time for the bell."

We had finally plowed our way through to the last chapter of *Great Expectations* and were about to wrap it up when Spike came in.

"Miss Davis, I've got an office full of parents down there and the battery has conked out on Miss Ledbetter's car. Do you have any team players in here you'd trust to send to the post office? Miss Ledbetter's got a registered letter she has to get on that one o'clock mail truck."

I knew there was something to that saying "clothes make the man" when Miss Davis said, "Pepper Junior, would you mind going?"

Spike frowned. "Fallon, why don't you keep her company?" he said.

Fallon rolled her eyes at Melinda Sue, but I noticed she didn't hesitate to close *Great Expectations*. "Since I think it's too hot to wear a coat inside, I'll have to go to my locker for mine, Miss Davis. Is that okay?"

If I hadn't been so well dressed in my gray slacks and cashmere sweater, I might have been a little worried about finding something to talk to Fallon about, but expensive clothes can't help but give you confidence. And like I'm always trying to tell Frankie, you just can't let people intimidate you.

We hadn't even walked a block before she asked me about my new outfit, just like I knew she would.

"When my dad gets his business established out here, I'm going to get one of those bunny coats," Fallon said. "The kind with the hood. I would have had it this year if Frankie Banning's dad weren't such an old meanie."

"What does your dad do?"

"Formerly, he was president of Super Bread, a division of BTT. Had a limousine and a chauffeur named Johnny and was always flying around in the company plane. He formerly had so much power everyone in the whole corporation was jealous."

Sounded to me as if "formerly" Fallon's old man got sacked.

"But he got tired of the rat race, and my mom's a painter and could hardly find any light in the city, so we moved out here. Daddy is selling real estate just until the city council approves the proposal for his business. You just can't imagine how Mr. Banning is holding back the progress of this town."

"I don't suppose your dad is considering opening a pizza parlor? I've got quite a bit of influence with Mr. Banning, and I could put in a good word."

"A pizza parlor? Really! My father was formerly a

very important man, and he can't be involved in anything tacky."

Fallon put her nose so far in the air, she didn't even
see Vic Terry's truck coming. I had to grab her arm
to keep her from walking off the curb right in front of
him. Her eyes looked awful shiny like they could have
tears in them, but none dripped so I decided I had
imagined it.

"Are you and Frankie going steady?"

I turned up the collar of my jacket so maybe she
would think my red color was only a reflection. I hate
it when my face steams up like that.

"Yeah."

"He's cute, but my dad would have a fit if I had
anything to do with him. Under the circumstances,
you understand?"

"Sure."

"Besides, I'm attracted to older men. Do you know
Don Carruthers?"

"Chub's big brother?"

"Yes, but he's nothing like Chub! Donnie plays tackle. He's a starter. Since Trenton Millbock left, every
girl in town is just nuts about Donnie."

"He came out to my house once."

"Pepper, everybody knows you tell lies! I don't believe that for a minute."

"We went for a ride in his car Halloween night.
That's a red Camaro he drives, isn't it?"

"That's just because my folks wouldn't allow me to invite any older kids to my party." She grabbed my arm. If her hands were dirty, and she got a spot on my jacket, I'd deck her. "Did he mention me? Tell me everything he said."

"He's got a pretty foul mouth. Not my type at all."

Mr. Terry was coming out of the post office with his mail when we started up the steps. He said, "Pepper, you look like Little Red Riding Hood this morning." I always did think Mr. Terry was a nice man.

The post mistress gave me ninety cents change when I mailed the letter. The sun was breaking through the clouds when we came outside. "Too pretty a day to waste in school. We've got enough left for a pack of cigarettes. Want to go down to the dock and have a smoke?"

"We have to give that money back to Mr. Spade! Besides, I think smoking makes a girl look tough. I don't think Donnie would want me to. Doesn't Frankie complain about your breath when you're making out?"

"At a time like that, who's thinking about your breath?"

Fallon checked her watch. I don't think she was in the mood to go back to school either.

"It's about time for lunch. We could walk over to my house and make sandwiches. Do you like peanut butter?"

"Will your dad be home?"

"Of course not. He'll be working. You don't think just because he was formerly a corporate executive, he's not keeping himself busy now, do you?"

"Look, Fallon, don't worry about it so much. Shoot, my dad's been fired lots of times, and he always gets it together again."

"And does just as well as he did before?"

"He bought me all these fine clothes, didn't he?"

Fallon's folks lived in a big white Victorian house on a corner lot. She said they bought such a big house so her mother could have a studio upstairs and her dad an office. We went in the back door, and Fallon was getting food out of the refrigerator when I first heard people talking upstairs and pretended I didn't.

"Scotch at eleven-thirty in the morning? That's terrific! Maybe on top of everything else you can become an alcoholic."

"Considering all the support I get from you, Ellen, it's a wonder I don't have a little nip for breakfast."

Fallon and I had done a good job concentrating on our sandwiches and ignoring the conversation, but when the door slammed so hard the kitchen light jiggled, our heads snapped up. I think we were both holding our breath as we listened to someone pounding down the back stairs.

Fallon's father looked as startled as we did when he came into the kitchen.

106

"Fallon, honey, I didn't know you had come home. How's my princess?" He kissed her on the cheek. "And who's this pretty girl? A new friend?"

"Daddy, this is Pepper Marlan. She just moved here from California."

"Pepper Junior." I stuck out my hand to shake his hand. "My name's Pepper Junior."

"Pepper Junior? Isn't that cute?" I was hoping he was going to leave, but he turned back. "Did you say Marlan? Do your folks own that five-acre piece out on the Sound?"

"My grandmother does."

"I don't suppose she's thinking of selling? Waterfront property is in great demand these days. I've been looking for a parcel about that size. I'm planning to put up some very tasteful condos."

"We're not considering selling. You see, my dad's probably going to be marrying a local woman and moving back here pretty soon. He and I've led an exciting life traveling around, but we're ready to settle down now. We're going to fix up Granny's house real nice and live there forever. I'll be inviting Fallon out to some parties we'll be giving."

"Well, if your grandmother should change her mind, I would appreciate it if you'd let me know. I have good connections in the city. Big money. We could make your grandmother a handsome offer."

Something hit the floor upstairs hard. We all looked up and got very quiet. I thought I could hear someone crying.

"Fallon, why don't you take Pepper Junior upstairs to meet your mother. Cheer her up. I don't think her painting is going well this morning, and I'm backed up. Meetings. A couple of big deals cooking. You understand?"

"Sure, Daddy."

I just dearly love peanut butter, but theirs must have been dry. It got stuck in my throat.

When Mr. O'Brien's car had pulled out of the drive, Fallon put her head down on the table and began to cry. I felt betrayed. The Fallon O'Briens of this world weren't supposed to have troubles that made them cry like everybody else.

"You got something in your eye?" I said to the top of her head.

"I think my parents are going to get a divorce. I just want to die."

"Now aren't you being silly? You think your folks are the only ones who ever have a spat? Why Frankie's mom and dad just fight like cats and dogs all the time. You think they're going to get a divorce?"

"Do they really?"

"Sure. When Frankie and I are making out in the living room, we can hear them throwing things around in the kitchen, yelling at each other. At first, even though they were just begging me to come for supper and stuff, I didn't even want to go, but like Frankie says, they've been going on like that as long as he can remember. That's just the way married people behave."

Fallon wiped her eyes with a paper napkin and began to shape up. "Do the Bannings really let you and Frankie kiss and stuff right in his house?"

"Almost every night."

"Gee, you're lucky, Pepper. I'd give anything if my parents would let me invite Donnie Carruthers over. His sister says she thinks he really likes me, but he's afraid I'm too young."

We were just a block from school when Fallon saw the red Camaro and about had a fit. "There he is! Pepper, that's Donnie driving and Pete Porter's with him. Jeff's brother. They must not have football practice this afternoon because of the night game. What're we going to do?"

"Swoon? Throw ourselves in front of the car? What do you want to do?"

"I want to talk to him. I bet they come around the block again. Can't you get them to stop?"

I didn't want them to stop. Chub's brother seemed like a pig to me, and if Pete were anything like ole Jeff, he belonged in *The Rocky Horror Picture Show* too. But Fallon was tugging on me, and I didn't want her to think I was a coward. So when they came back around cruising slow, I yelled, "Taxi!" They stopped, but then Fallon wouldn't go over to the car, even though I was trying to shove her in that direction since I thought that was the purpose of getting those freaky guys to stop in the first place.

"You girls want to take a little ride?" You could tell Chub's brother really thought he was hot stuff. He had a pouting look around his mouth and kept one eyebrow permanently arched. He didn't look cool like Rocky Rivers—he looked spoiled.

"I don't think we should, do you Pepper?"

I just wished Fallon would make up her mind. Those guys looked like nerds to me, but if they turned her on, I'd help her out. The car was okay, and English was over. I didn't care about missing any of the other classes.

"Okay," I said and started walking toward the school.

"You afraid you can't control yourself?" That must have been Jeff's brother. They had the same horse laugh.

Fallon grabbed my arm. "Well, Pepper, if you really want to, I guess we can. Just around the block." She got in the front seat, and I had a devil of a time scrunching into the back. She was so busy grinning at Donnie Carruthers, she didn't offer to raise the back of her seat.

I sat way over against the window so I could watch the scenery. Pete wasn't the greatest conversationalist, and I was wondering if Frankie would be worried when I didn't turn up for history. Fallon wasn't saying much either. She was spending all of her time giggling at every dopey thing Donnie said. I didn't get worried until he pulled a skinny little cigarette out of his pocket and made a big deal about lighting it. He had his window down, and that grass was so loosely packed I was afraid an ash would blow back and burn my new jacket. Fallon was pretending she didn't know what he was smoking, but if that girl had lived in Manhattan and didn't recognize that smell, she had spent her time in an iron lung.

"Come on, Fallon, take one drag. I'll take care of you. You won't feel a thing from just one puff, promise. I've had a lot of experience with this stuff," Carruthers, the creep, said.

"Donnie, only if you promise you won't let anything bad happen to me." Fallon took hold of it like it was a lizard that would bite. "Is this right, Donnie?" I believed her until she pulled in on that weed, and took enough of that smoke into her lungs to fly the Goodyear Blimp. She didn't even cough.

"Oh, Donnie, I feel so fuzzy . . . and dizzy. I think I might float right out of this car. What am I going to do?"

"I'll hang on to you Fallon." Donnie put his arm around her and tucked her under his arm. Fallon hid her face in his chest. "We wouldn't want a pretty little thing like you to get away, would we, Pete?" Donnie looked in the rearview mirror and began to laugh in a mean superior-sounding way. "How you doin' back there, ole buddy?" He rolled his eyes at the top of Fallon's head to indicate what the standard for winning was.

"Give Pepper a drag." Fallon's voice was muffled into Donnie's shirt.

I had tried grass down at the video parlor once when Rocky and those guys he hung out with had been on a roll and bought some from Freaky Freddie. When I heard how much it cost was when I decided it didn't do anything for me I couldn't do without. Like I was always telling Zack, we had more important places to put our money. He agreed with me, most of the time.

"You want one?" Pete said. He wasn't very enthusiastic. Pete and I were just along for the ride.

"No. That's kid stuff. Out in California where I come from, we went through that stage ages ago." I never thought I would be anxious to get back to school, but Donnie was heading out of town, and I wasn't eager to take a long scenic drive in the country with Pete, no matter how much Fallon liked Donnie. Even though there was no chemistry working for us, I knew ole lover boy Donnie would start harassing Pete to show his manliness and rip my new clothes off or something. Guys like Donnie need company to keep up their courage.

"You ever see Matt Dillon out there?"

"He was in my homeroom. When he wasn't off on location."

"No shit! Guess he's really cool, huh? Girls panting all over him?"

"Gay as pink ink."

"You're crazy! That guy's the new John Wayne. You see *The Outsiders?*"

Pete was edging over the boundary line I'd set in the backseat, and that stupid Donnie was turning down a country road. I had to keep our dumb conversation going or Pete was going to be all over my new jacket.

"You think having muscles exempts a guy from the gay bars? Ever watch the Oakland Raiders? Thirty percent."

"You're nuts. People from California always are. The Raiders are jocks. Matt Dillon's a stud."

"He told me all about it once. Said when he was young and began to ask his folks about sex, they sent him to camp. Boys' camp. It really messed him up."

Donnie was kissing Fallon and not watching the road. We veered off and hit the side of the drainage ditch before he whipped the car back and almost cracked our necks. He was driving down a dirt right-of-way road that cut through the potato fields back to the Sound just like the one that led to Granny's. I wished he were taking me home, and Frankie would be waiting for me in our beach house, but that bluff up ahead didn't lead to our beach. The closer we got to the water, the faster Donnie was driving. One cigarette surely couldn't have made even a bozo like him think this car could fly.

"Oh, Donnie, be careful. I'm scared." I don't think Fallon was flirting. I think she was worried. I know I was. He was driving like a maniac. "Pepper and I better get back to school. I think lunch must be over."

I wished she had thought of that when we were still in town. Liking a guy can really mess up a girl's head, even somebody like Fallon, I guess. The road ended at the edge of the bluff, and Donnie was still barreling it when the water came into view. Fallon covered her face and screamed, but if I were going out, I wanted to know what was happening all the way. I grabbed the back of Donnie's seat and held on tight as I could. Pete wasn't saying a word. Guys can't. But he was bracing himself and he looked white. Donnie hit the brakes and the front end of that Camaro skidded from side to side like a fan. I fell back against the seat, and it didn't feel as if I had any bones holding me up. We all laughed because we weren't dead, I guess.

When Donnie ripped that car into reverse and shot down that road backward, I felt as if I were in one of those horror movies where they overdo the special effects. I didn't know a car would work that fast going the wrong way. Fallon was crying and begging him to stop, and Pete had this stupid grin on his face that showed he was more scared than happy. He was sitting on the edge of his seat whipping his head back to look out of the rear window, but he was clutching the back of the passenger seat for dear life. There was a shed on the edge of the field on my side, and I thought I saw a man on a tractor, but as fast as we were moving I could have been mistaken. When Donnie bounced the car to a stop and jerked the shift forward, I had this sinking feeling this madness wasn't ever going to stop.

"Don't worry kiddos, I'm better than Cale Yarborough. Watch this."

Don't ask me how we stopped again, but even though the long hood seemed to be hanging out in space, the wheels were on the ground, but right on the edge of the embankment. Fallon jumped out with Pete and me right behind her. One minute Donnie was leaning against the door looking at us with a big macho grin on his face, and the next minute the bank began to give way. A big hunk of clay went first and then a slide started. Donnie grabbed the wheel and rode the Camaro down until it crashed into a big boulder right at the edge of the beach. The grille folded in and the hood popped up. Steam was shooting all over the place. For a second the three of us stood there frozen with the stupidest looks on our faces. I don't think we moved an eyelash until Donnie started swearing. He had jumped out and

115

was clutching his head and doing a jig by the side of his crumpled car. His face looked like one of those pictures of people who survived Nagasaki.

The bank was only about twelve or fifteen feet high, so when we got our wits back, we scrambled down to him, all of us yelling, "Are you okay? Are you hurt?"

"Look at that son-of-a-bitching car! My dad's gonna kill me." Donnie picked up rocks off the beach and pelted the car. While he was punishing the Camaro, the three of us jerked our heads up listening to what couldn't be anything but a police siren. Life just hadn't prepared Fallon for trouble. I thought she was going to faint before she threw her arms around my neck and hid her face.

"Don't worry, Fallon. We're okay. Nobody's hurt," I said.

"But, Pepper, what is everyone going to say?"

"What in the hell's going on down there?" Charlie Adams took off his Smokey the Bear hat as if he hoped it were distorting his vision. Vic Terry was with him. I guess that was who I had seen in the shed back there.

Donnie, Pete, and Fallon jumped in the backseat so fast I didn't have any choice but to ride back into town in the hot seat between Charlie and Vic.

"Girl, who're your folks?" Charlie asked. "I bet you're going to catch it when they find out you were joyriding with that clown." He nodded at Donnie, the clown in the backseat who looked as if he might cry.

"I'm an orphan, just passing through."

Vic Terry laughed. I was glad he could see the humor in this situation. It certainly was eluding me.

"Charlie, don't you know Zack Marlan's kid?"

He shook his head and said, "It figures."

We didn't say much till they had us all lined up in Spike's office, and then nobody had a chance because Spike was making speeches. I think he would have been better in a huddle where no one but the team would have to listen.

Fallon was crying like crazy, which wasn't a bad ploy because they spent the time trying to get her to shut up rather than grilling us, but then she blew it. "I want Miss Davis in here," she said.

Oh, great! Miss Davis would never marry Zack if these bozos convinced her I was a juvenile delinquent.

"Your parents, that's who we're going to get in here," Spike said, but he sent Miss Ledbetter to find Miss Davis too. "They're going to see what I go through trying to turn these scruffy sandlot delinquents into pros. Yes sir, they are."

"Mine aren't home," Pete said.

"This telephone will ring out to the oyster factory. Their shift doesn't end until four. We'll find them, don't you worry."

"Spike, I guess I better search them," Charlie said.

I thought surely even someone as dumb as Donnie would have had sense enough to have gotten rid of his grass, but I could tell by the sick look on his face he hadn't. Spike hadn't missed that look either.

"Oh, well, Charlie, I don't think that's necessary. They were just joyriding. Not that we're not going to make them sorry they ever saw that car, mind you, but Pete and Donnie are on the team. They wouldn't have anything on 'em."

Miss Davis came to the door, looked around, and slipped into a place against the wall next to Vic Terry.

"Well, Spike, if your team's so clean, then they don't have nothing to worry about, do they? All four of you, face the wall. Lean on your hands above your head. Spread eagle."

"Oh, I just can't!" Fallon was wailing into her hands covering her face.

"Miss Davis, you frisk the girls," Charlie said.

"Oh, for heavensakes," Miss Davis said. "Fallon, don't cry honey, it's okay."

"Well, well, what've we got here?" Charlie was looking at the two joints he had found in Donnie's pocket with the glee of a Vegas gambler watching four oranges roll up.

"I didn't have any." Pete's voice quivered. Donnie and Fallon both looked at me, waiting for me to join the ranks of the squealers. They must have been nuts if they thought I wanted to team up with Pete. Miss Davis wasn't talking, but she wasn't missing anything either.

"How did this all happen?" Miss Davis asked the first sensible question. Spike had just been spouting his version, and he hadn't even been there. It just burned me up. "You girls went to the post office, and then what?" Miss Davis at least looked at us like we weren't scum, even if she did have that disappointed look people get.

"We were just riding around minding our own business, and these girls stopped us," Pete said.

"Who stopped you?" Spike said.

"Pepper."

When Fallon dropped her eyes and Spike smiled, that's when I realized I was in trouble.

"Like father, like . . . daughter," Spike said.

"I think you better get Frankie," I whispered to Miss Davis. She left the room without a word.

By the time Frankie and Miss Davis got back, Spike had Fallon on the phone, and she was saying, "Oh, Daddy, I'm so sorry, and I'm so scared."

She didn't look any more scared than Frankie. I didn't know how much Miss Davis had told him, but they hadn't had much time, and he was looking around the room as if he were confused. Then a strange thing happened. He looked angry. Ohmigod, if he were getting jealous of Pete, I might as well put on a ball and chain.

I moved over next to him and took hold of his arm. "Frankie I *need* you!" I whispered.

"Okay, Marlan, you're next," Spike said. "Get on the phone."

"We don't have a phone. Besides my grandmother's past eighty and too old to get involved in this."

"You should have thought of that when you started all this trouble," Spike said. "You've got to have somebody."

"I think we better call my sister," Frankie said so low I don't know how they heard him.

"Banning, where in the hell did you come from?" Spike said. "Which sister?"

I held my breath, hoping Frankie would get it right.

"Lydia." He ducked his head. I began to breathe normally.

"Lydia? Well now isn't that rich? Lydia Banning coming to bat for Zack Marlan's kid?" Spike had a filthy laugh. He dialed the number and held out the phone. "Which one of you is going to tell her what she's in for?"

"I will," I said. "Lydia? This is Pepper Junior Marlan. Yes. I'm in Mr. Spade's office down at the high school. No, I haven't gone out for football. I'm in a little trouble. You see this clown cracked up his car . . . no, I'm okay. It kind of slipped into the Sound." I was trying to play it straight for Spike, but that Lydia was nutty. She was getting the biggest kick out of the whole thing. I was having visions of being handcuffed by the narcs, and she was poking fun at Spike. "Lydia, I was just wondering if you didn't have anything else to do . . . Frankie and I were kind of wondering if you could come down here? Gee, thanks a lot, Lydia."

Nine

Miss Davis must have known I was watching Fallon and Pepper rather than paying attention to how Pip, Estella, and Old Joe met their great expectations and lived happily ever after, but she didn't call me down for it. In fact, she glanced out the window and then smiled at me like she was pleased as I was that Pepper and Fallon seemed to be making it just fine.

I think maybe I really began to relax for the first time since Pepper arrived. My girl, all wrapped up in spiffy warm clothes, was doing a responsible job for the principal with the most popular girl in school. Knowing Pepper, they would probably be running around together by the time they got back. Everything was going to turn out all right after all, just like in *Great Expectations.*

At lunch I waited around for a while, but when Pepper didn't show up, I wasn't concerned. I was hoping maybe Fallon had taken her home to eat something. It would do Pepper good to spend some time with a nice family like the O'Briens. In history I don't sit by the windows, but I asked the teacher if I could move because I had to watch for someone, which wasn't a lie.

When I caught sight of Pepper's red jacket, she looked like a red rubber ball bouncing down the street. I was so happy. I started listening real hard to Mr. Walker's lecture to make up for having let my mind wander through the first part. But I couldn't get the drift, so I sneaked another look out the window just in time to see Pepper cup her hands and call something to some guys in a red car that looked like Donnie Carruthers'. I began to get a sour taste in my mouth. Didn't she know Fallon would be so embarrassed she would never have anything to do with her again? Spike would kill her if she didn't get in here. The car stopped. It was that jerk-off Donnie. I took a breath and felt guilty when Pepper walked a few steps toward the school. Pepper was my girl. She wouldn't have anything to do with those creeps. But Fallon had stopped.

I was sending Pepper ESP messages. Come on Pepper. Just one more block. If you don't get yourself in this schoolhouse right this minute, I'm going to come out there and drag you by the hair, after I destroy those freaks in that red car.

Pepper and Fallon were talking. Holding a conference to decide if they were going to wreck my faith in the human race. Cripes, Fallon was running across the street toward the car, and that Pepper Marlan who you can't trust out of your sight was going right along with her. What can a guy expect from a woman who used to ride with a bike gang in California?

I couldn't swallow. It felt as if I had a tennis ball in my throat. I wanted to get out of that class, but after everyone had found out Pepper was going with that creep, I didn't want them to remember I couldn't take it. I didn't watch them drive off. I had enough evidence to know you can never count on women. I decided I would join the merchant marine. Lie about my age, and try to get into submarines. Tell them I didn't care if I ever surfaced.

Science must have been about half over when Miss Davis came to get me. I hadn't been paying much attention. I was trying to decide if I would write Pepper one letter and mail it when our sub took supplies off Africa or New Zealand, or if I would just let her always wonder what had happened to me.

"Pepper's in trouble," Miss Davis said when she got me out in the hall.

"So what else is new?"

"Frankie don't give up on her now. She needs you."

"That's not what it looked like outside a little while ago. When she got in a car with some thugs."

"Don't be a little twerp, Frankie. This could be serious!"

I followed Miss Davis down the hall, but I was kind of dragging my feet. She was fiddling with something on a chain around her neck.

"I think she's getting framed down there." Miss Davis pressed that thing around her neck, which looked like a ring, up against her lips.

"What's that?"

She dropped it. Put it inside her shirt.

"An engagement ring."

"Why are you wearing it around your neck?"

"I wanted to find a way to tell Pepper I was getting married before I just sprung it on her. You understand?"

She knew. She had seen through Pepper's campaign to get Miss Davis to marry her dad. I never would understand women.

I hadn't known what to expect when we walked into Spike's office, but I sure wasn't prepared for a scene out of "Hill Street Blues." Donnie Carruthers had misplaced any cool he had ever had. The wimp all doubled over in his chair, picking his thumbnail, wasn't that ox who broke heads on the football field. And Pete

Porter looked as if he knew what it was like to be scared for a change. Fallon had lost a little luster too.

Charlie Adams, fingering the head of his pistol. Vic Terry. What in the devil were they doing in Spike's office?

Then I looked at Pepper. She was a raccoon again. One glance and I knew I was done for. I was going to be saddled with trying to take care of this screwy girl the rest of my life.

Calling Lydia seemed to be just what Pepper wanted me to do, but I was uneasy. Lydia was so unpredictable. But I'd rather have gone to jail myself than call Mom or Dad.

I heard her screech to a stop out in front and hoped Charlie hadn't heard. She couldn't be very effective as a responsible adult for Pepper while she was trying to talk Charlie out of a speeding ticket.

Lydia once had wanted to be an actress. I think she would have been good at it. There was no mischief in her eyes when she and Meg Blake came into that crowded office. Lydia even shook hands with Spike, and I know what she thinks of him. I don't know how she had had time to dress for the part, but she was wearing a navy blue suit and white lace at her neck, which made her look sincere and reliable.

Bringing Meg Blake along was an interesting touch, but I wondered if that couldn't backfire on us. Meg's a lady lawyer I'm not sure Port of Egypt is ready for yet.

Next to arrive were Mr. and Mrs. O'Brien, looking as if they had just strolled in off of Park Avenue. At the sight of them, Fallon burst into tears. One got on each side of her, and you could just tell they had a united front.

"Gentlemen, whatever has happened here, I am certain we can straighten it out. My wife and I have a great deal of faith in this community, don't we, darling? I was very well-connected in Manhattan, but I gave it all up because I thought my wife and daughter could have a more wholesome environment living out here with good people like you. Right, Ellen?"

"Yes, darling."

Pepper's lip twitched in the strangest way. For a minute I was terrified, thinking she was going to grin at this inappropriate time, but she looked down, and the twitch went away.

When Mike Carruthers came in with blood on his butcher's apron and shoved Donnie up against the wall, taking on something awful about the little bastard having wrecked a ten-thousand dollar automobile, Spike decided it was time to sort out the players. Miss Davis and I got sent to the bench outside in the main office.

Right after the final bell rang, Lydia came out, winked at me, and asked to use Miss Ledbetter's phone.

"Hi Mom, it's Lydia. Listen, Harvey has a Rotary dinner tonight, I stuck the kids with a sitter, and I was wondering if you would mind if I took Frankie and Pepper out to eat? Good. You'll let Mis' Marlan know? Okay. Sure I'll tell him to mind his manners, Mom."

She rolled her eyes at me and went back there where everyone was talking awful loud.

About five o'clock Miss Davis looked at her watch and said, "Frankie, will you call me if I can do anything for Pepper? I should go home. Dan always calls me before he leaves his office."

"Sure."

"Dan's my fiancé. You understand?"

"That's okay. Lydia's pretty good in a scrap. She's had lots of practice with my dad."

To be honest, I was relieved when Miss Davis left. We had pretty much worn out any topics you can discuss with a teacher.

About five-thirty, Vic Terry came out.

"Got to get home to feed my pigs," he said.

Miss Ledbetter had left with Miss Davis. By six o'clock, I was feeling downright ashamed of myself. Here Pepper was in there probably getting sent to Sing Sing, and my stomach was growling. All I could think about was pork chops and Mom's fudge cake.

Finally the O'Briens came out. Mrs. O'Brien was muttering something under her breath to Mr. O'Brien that sounded like "you damned fool," but Fallon smiled at me and said, "Goodnight, Frankie, see you in English tomorrow."

It hurt my conscience to be disloyal to a nice girl like Fallon, but I couldn't figure out what I had ever seen in her.

Pepper, Meg, and Lydia came out of Spike's office looking as proper as Sunday school teachers, until we were in the car. Then I swear they acted like they were the Three Stooges. All talking at once, punching each other and laughing. Lydia couldn't even drive. She put her forehead on the steering wheel and giggled.

"Meg, you sounded like Mike Hammer questioning that dodo Donnie," Pepper said.

"No, it was his dad's fist in his face that broke that kid."

"Yeah, like a big red smoked ham."

"The judge will have to charge him for possession, but Spike can probably get him probation," Meg said.

"He'll get worse from his dad," Lydia said.

"I'd probably have gotten life, if you hadn't kept reminding Spike that Donnie was the instigator and we had to remember the team," Pepper said.

"What did you get?" I was finally able to ask.

"A good tongue lashing and two weeks of detention. Fallon, the fink, only got one week because she never would admit going with those guys was her idea."

"Maybe you should have ratted on her, Pepper," Meg said.

"A stoolie? It'd take more than Fallon O'Brien."

"Maybe her hundred percent pure reputation will be slightly soiled though," Lydia said. "When I was in school, phonies like Fallon gave me a rash."

"So what's changed?" Meg said as we stopped to drop her at her office.

"Thanks a ton, Meg," Pepper said. "I hear they don't let you smoke in reform school."

"Saving wayward girls is my favorite kind of case." Meg winked at Pepper and walked toward her office, whistling.

"Where do you kids want to eat? The Hotel? Soundfront? I'm feeling generous," Lydia said.

"I don't suppose you know any place where they have pizza?" Pepper said.

Lydia laughed. "If you promise not to tell Dad, we can go to Mario's in Northold. That's not a long drive, and he makes wonderful minestrone soup too."

"If I'm going to eat out in a real restaurant, I'm not having soup!" Pepper said.

Lydia ordered a beer and I was relieved when Pepper wanted a large Pepsi. I was glad she's only addicted to cigarettes. Lydia talked Pepper into trying oysters to start, but she ate them with her eyes closed. I thought maybe a large pizza was too much, even if it is her favorite food, but she said she would take home anything that was left. She liked it cold and she wanted her grandmother to taste it.

Mario's faces the bay, and you can see the lights of Shelter Island sparkling in the distance. Pepper didn't appreciate the view or talk much until she had eaten more pizza than I had ever seen anyone tackle in one sitting, but then the view got her attention.

"I'm not in any hurry. Harvey can relieve the sitter. Why don't I have another cup of coffee and you guys have dessert? Let's enjoy the scene."

Between bites of her fudge brownie with ice cream and caramel sauce, Pepper said, "Lydia, you should have been a lawyer. You were better in Spike's office this afternoon than Meg."

"I thought about it once before I decided I'd rather dance in the Follies." She grinned, but then she looked out at the lights twinkling on the water, and her face turned serious. "I just know those characters better than Meg does. Spike had a terrific crush on me in high school. You can't imagine how jealous he was of your father. Zack always beat him at everything."

"I don't see why they ever made him principal," I said.

"I know what you mean. I've always thought I could thank Spike for Harvey's deciding we had to send Trenton away to school. Spike always expected him to get into jams, and Trenton never let him down."

"I always wondered why Dad didn't send me away,

so he wouldn't have to watch me not playing sports and stuff."

"You're okay, Frankie."

"You'd have been ashamed to call me your brother if you'd known how much I wanted to deck Donnie and Pete this afternoon."

Lydia's eyes flicked from Pepper to me, and she smiled. Of course I had to blush like a dope.

"Little brother, I think you've been growing up while we weren't watching." She picked up the check and took out her American Express card Mom says she uses too freely. "You kids want anything else?"

"Yes."

I couldn't believe Pepper could eat another bite without exploding.

"If you wouldn't mind, I'd like to know about you and my dad."

Ohmigod!

"Frankie, are you ready for this?" Lydia asked.

"Sure," I said trying not to gulp like an idiot. I think Mario must have turned up the thermostat. I was hot all over. Pepper was cool, just sat there calmly waiting with her hands clasped in front of her on the table.

"Well, we fell in love when we were kids. Your grandmother and Zack were having a hard time making it after your grandfather died, but I was too young to realize how bad it was, and your grandmother tried so hard for Zack to have a carefree life. She should have made him pay more attention to the truck farm, but he wanted to play football, and she couldn't refuse him anything. I didn't help. Dances, parties, clothes, cars—all that stuff was terribly important to me then. Things I just assumed everyone could afford. One night we went dancing at the Rainbow Room. Took the bus. While we were dancing, I remember him saying I was made out of flesh, flowers, and razor blades."

Lydia shook her head, folded a matchbook cover into an accordion. "I'd rather not think how he paid that check. Dad kept me at home for a month because we missed the last bus and had to get a ride with the bread truck the next morning. We had always planned to get married after high school. Too impatient to be together to bother with college." She chuckled. "We were going to Florida to get jobs on a cruise ship and see the world. The wealthy widows would have loved Zack. He had a way with women."

Lydia looked so sad I got a lump in my throat. You just never think about older women like Lydia ever having been in love. Feeling like I did about Pepper. Especially not your sister.

"Then we had an argument about something. I don't even remember what anymore. Zack had a lot of pride, so to show me he didn't give a damn, he went over to East Hampton and got a summer job. To show *him* I didn't give a damn, I finally started accepting dates with Harvey Millbock, who had been after me forever.

133

And made damn sure Zack knew about it. In about a week Zack came strutting over on the ferry with a blonde who worked in a bar where she met these guys from Vegas."

I'd never seen Pepper sit so still. Lydia lit a cigarette and watched the smoke drift up, but Pepper never took her eyes off Lydia's face.

"I'd been pregnant for a month when he left, but my periods are irregular, and I've always been careless. Just ask Dad about my carelessness. Then I got a letter from Zack saying he had gotten into a little trouble trying to make some money for us to get to Florida on and he had to leave for a while, but he would send for me. I had known all along the blonde was only to pay me back for Harvey, but the Vegas collectors are very good. They bribed the captain of the fishing boat he was shipping on. Dad was very generous. Didn't ask your grandmother to take off a dollar from what she asked him for the truck farm. And since Harvey was willing to take me off his hands two and half months pregnant, he even helped finance dental school. God knows Trenton and I have always tried to be grateful."

Tears were spilling out of Pepper's eyes, running down her chin. Lydia used the linen napkin.

"Trenton knows?" I couldn't believe it. He called Harvey 'Dad,' the best I could remember.

"Oh, I promised I wouldn't tell. None of them know I did. But as hard as he tries, Harvey just can't feel about Trenton the way he does about the girls. Those gray eyes of Trenton's? Red flags to Harvey, I guess. I had to let Trenton know it was what I'd done, not him. So Trenton and I have our little secret. Now you two are my partners in crime. But if I don't get you home, you're going to be in more trouble, and I would imagine you've both had enough for one day. Right?"

Lydia put on her coat, started to stand up, but Pepper reached out to her.

"Just one more thing, Lydia. . . ."

"No, your dad doesn't know, and I'll pull out your fingernails one by one, if you ever tell him."

Lydia put her arm around Pepper as she walked to the car. "I know that'll be tough for you, Pepper, but I knew you'd hear the gossip while you're here, and I had hoped you could hear it straight. From me. Just like Trenton did. I'm glad you asked."

I wished I could have read Pepper's mind as we drove home. She was awful quiet, just sat there hugging her doggy bag of pizza and looking straight ahead. I put my arm around her shoulders. I don't think Lydia even noticed. We all had lots on our minds.

Funny, I wasn't shocked about Lydia and Zack Marlan. Nobody had ever told me the story, but it was like I had always known, and she had just made it all right for me to admit to knowing. I felt sorry for Lydia, but then I think she's the kind of woman who probably enjoys having a lurid past.

"I'm going to dump you bums here." Lydia stopped her Mercedes at the road leading up to Pepper's house. "Frankie, you can walk Pepper home. It'd be a shame to waste a moon like that."

Lydia can be okay. No matter what Dad says.

We got out, and I took Pepper's hand, but she broke away and ran back to Lydia's side of the car.

"Thanks, for the pizza . . . and everything."

"It was worth it, Pepper."

"And, Lydia, red's my favorite color."

She knew! I'd never understand women.

"You're looking good." Lydia whirled around and headed toward town too fast.

Ten

If Lydia hadn't come to my defense, I'd probably be doing hard time in reform school over the holidays. From the moment she walked into Spike's office, I knew my troubles were over. When I was a dumb little kid I used to dream about finding a mother who would cook us good meals, read me stories, and plan birthday parties. I used to look around in the park, thinking I'd find someone I could take home to Zack. But in my best dreams, there was no one like Lydia. Funny, pretty, smart. And kind. But not in a way that makes me feel as if I owe her something. I can't stand that. Miss Davis is nice, but she doesn't make me laugh. And Miss Davis will never have courage like Lydia, who'd stand up to the Godfather if she had to. Together? Shoot, I bet me and Lydia could take on the Russians.

But some things are too good to be true, I guess. Besides, I'm probably lucky Lydia and Zack didn't get together. Zack has given me enough trouble. The two of them would probably been more than I could have managed. Not that I don't think Lydia is terrific, but she has some nutty ideas and she doesn't know when she's well off. That woman has a Mercedes car sleek and slick as silk. Plastic money? She could buy the Golden Gate Bridge, sign for it, and charge it to one of a bundle of cards in her wallet. And smart as she is, I think the only work Lydia has is being a rebel. It's not my place to spoil her fun, but if in her daydreams she ever sees Zack wrapping her in a mink coat and filling her refrigerator with ham and Budweiser beer, her memory is bad.

Oh, Zack and I've had some swell times, like when we took off for a weekend in Mexico and stayed six weeks because we could get a fistful of pesos for our dollars. Could have stayed longer if that Maria hadn't cleaned out Zack's wallet while he was sleeping. And that stick job he had in that Vegas casino for a while that came with a swanky room and all the breakfast we could eat. If only Zack wouldn't have listened to Mike Riley's plan for breaking the bank, I could have gone to school there, made some friends. Women and a short cut to easy street, that's what's always dis-

138

tracting Zack. Granny has a way of making you feel like nothing gives her as much pleasure as doing for you. Maybe Zack got in the habit of expecting everyone to be like Granny.

From the way it looks, easy street must be lined with dentists' offices like Harvey Millbock's. Lydia's better off being a holy terror on the North Fork and looking at Zack's picture in her high school yearbook. I can't quite imagine Lydia sharing Tick's room in Oakland.

That night after Donnie Carruthers tried to kill us in his Camaro, when Lydia took us for pizza, I wrote something in my notebook that I read every day, and now I'm going to turn it into an essay for Miss Davis. "A friend is someone who knows everything there is to know about you and likes you just the same." I thought of that because that's the way it is for Frankie and me. We're going to be okay. For a few minutes in Spike's office, when I realized he thought I had been two-timing him with that coward Pete Porter, I about died, but we've got it all squared away now. Lydia likes to joke around, but she's not a dope. She knew we needed some time to talk, so she worked it so Frankie could walk me home. I promised him I would never like anyone else, and he kissed me all over my face, even my eyelids. Said he didn't want to miss one spot.

I floated into the house and wrote that line about

friends while I warmed up the pizza with anchovies, sausage, peppers, and extra cheese for Granny. She thought it was really interesting, but since she can't eat much before she goes to bed, I had to finish it.

Miss Davis wants us to write an essay describing an abstraction. She said we should try to define fuzzy feelings into something clear and straight. I thought about trying to tell how it feels to discover late in life that you have kind of a brother, but then I realized I might be betraying Lydia, even if I made my abstraction sort of vague.

Thinking about Trenton can drive me nuts. Sometimes I'm trying to imagine him, and I realize what I'm seeing is that old school picture of Zack that Granny keeps by her bed. My favorite image is the four of us walking down a beach with the waves rolling in. We're swinging along with our arms wrapped around each other's backs. I'm between Zack and Trenton, who's tall with wide shoulders, but I can't put a face on him that makes him look like Lydia and Zack both. Maybe when he comes home at Christmas I can make friends with him. Unless he blames Zack for a bunch of stuff, like having to go to military school. I don't expect him to treat me like a sister or anything, but I can always use another friend.

Fallon's not talking to me again, but I don't care. Her grandmother got sick the night of Donnie's accident, or so the story goes anyway, and she and her mother had to leave town for a week. By the time she came back, some kids had vandalized the locker room and sprayed obscenities on the gym floor, so no one was talking much about our trouble. But she still pretends I have never been to her house or anything, even though her dad wrote Granny a letter about buying our five acres. Granny and I didn't even give his letter a second thought. My traveling days are over, and we wouldn't sell our house for anything. Frankie, Granny, and I are too busy planning for Christmas to worry about Fallon O'Brien or her father.

Frankie and I have been trying to find a way to buy Granny a TV. When I have to go off to school, I think Phil Donahue might be good company for her. Mr. Banning said we could set up a stand along the road and sell all the Christmas trees we could cut out of his woods. But he thinks we should be planning to buy a kerosene heater so Granny wouldn't have to go out in the weather to collect wood for her fire. I promised myself I would do a better job of getting the wood in at night and get her a TV. The trouble is, cutting those trees is harder than we expected.

At night we've been making baskets out of pinecones, and Granny declares she sure would like to find one of them under her tree, but since she watches us fix them, that wouldn't be much of a surprise. We are going to give one to Mrs. Banning, Miss Davis, and Frankie's sisters, all except Lydia. We're doing a fancy ashtray out of beach glass for her, if we can get the glass to stick.

Where we are going to make a killing, if I can keep Granny from giving them all away, is with gingerbread houses. Zack moved in with Bea, so since he doesn't have to pay Tick any rent, he sent us twenty-five dollars. When Mrs. Banning told me how much those houses were bringing at the folk art shop, I invested Zack's money in supplies, and Granny and I have gone into business. The way I figure it, we'll make four dollars and eighty-five cents on each one, that's counting those Granny didn't charge for.

I'm real discouraged with my present for Frankie. I've been looking in the mirror and trying to draw my portrait. Looking at yourself hours on end can get to be a creepy experience. Granny thinks it's beginning to resemble me, especially around the eyes, but sometimes I think it looks like Gravel Gertie.

The day our essays were due to Miss Davis, I was checking mine over for spelling when Chub Carruthers passed me a note that said:

Hey Bluehead,
If you want to have a Christmas party, I suppose I could bring a turkey since Dad ordered more than he's going to sell. But I'd have to tell my folks I was coming to Frankie's house since it was your fault my brother wrecked his car.
"Chuck"

142

I wrote on the bottom:

I'll have to check my social calendar. Frankie and
I are in great demand during this season. Hold
on to the turkey until I let you know. Your brother
is a liar!
Pepper Junior

Chub has tried all sorts of ways to sweet-talk his
way back into my good graces since he miscast *Elizabeth and Essex*, but I'm still playing hard-to-get with
him. I think he comes from a whole family of dunder-
heads.

I thought Miss Davis had seen me passing the note
when she asked me to stay after class. Frankie stuck
around too, checking to see if I were in trouble I guess.

"Sit down, Pepper Junior. I'll write passes for you
kids to get to your next class."

"What's up, Miss Davis?"

"Oh, I haven't had a chance to talk to you lately,
and I just wondered how you were doing. Are you still
marking the days off your calendar until you can go
back to California?"

"I'm super. And marking that calendar got to be
depressing when I realized how fast the time was going.
So I'm making some big changes in my life. I'm going
to stay here."

I smiled at Frankie. He looked embarrassed, but he
grinned.

"Because my granny needs me and things."

"I'm glad to hear that Pepper. We would certainly miss you. Mr. Staff tells me he thinks you have natural musical talent, and I can see an improvement in your writing."

"Thanks, Miss Davis. Wait until you read this essay. It's terrific."

"I'm going to be making some big changes in my life too, Pepper Junior, and I wanted to tell you personally. . . . You see when I was in college, I met a man named Dan Bates. And we fell in love."

"Well, where is he?"

"He joined a law firm in New York this year. We just see each other on weekends. We're going to be married next summer. I wanted to tell you because I thought you might have had an idea that . . ."

"I wanted you to marry my dad? Yeah, I did toss that idea around for a while. Because he's such a neat guy and all."

"I'm sorry, Pepper. If I hadn't already met Dan, who knows what might have happened? And I'm flattered that you thought about me."

"Oh, that's all right, Miss Davis. Frankie and I've uncovered some stuff that might make it complicated for Zack to come back here to live anyway. It could be better for everyone concerned if he just visited Granny and me."

Miss Davis started to write passes for us when I had a super idea.

"How would you and Mr. Bates like to come to a party Frankie and I are probably going to have?"

Frankie's head jerked up since I hadn't had an opportunity to tell him about my idea.

"Our tree is going to be the best one in the county. You see, my grandfather whittled all the ornaments, and Granny says if we're real careful maybe one night we can put candles on it and light them. We're going to have a turkey and gingerbread and everything. Chub Carruthers might have to come, but that'll be okay."

"Unfortunately, we are going to spend the holidays with Dan's parents in Princeton, but I wish we could come. Your tree sounds beautiful."

She handed me the passes, and Frankie and I were at the door when she said, "Pepper Junior, I know I missed something not having you for a daughter."

I felt good about that the rest of the day.

"What did Miss Davis mean about you being musical?" Frankie said.

"Didn't you take those tests at the beginning of school?"

"Yes, and Mr. Staff wouldn't let me in the chorus. Mom was awful disappointed."

"Frankie, if you sing real loud—you know, like Lover

Boy—nobody can hardly tell if you're carrying the tune or not. We'll practice in our beach house."

"Why is Mr. Staff impressed with you?"

"He thinks it's some big deal because I can play things by ear. When Zack and I ran a bar for a while, there was a piano we used to fool around with. Zack loves to harmonize and clown it up. He thought we should put together an act, but we couldn't even agree on our name."

"What did he want to call your group?"

"Bingo and the Baby Beatnick, which you have to admit is yucky, even if it weren't outdated and I were a baby. But what I'd really like to play is a guitar. A real syrupy guitar. But the school doesn't have any string instruments."

"I suppose if you had a guitar, you'd have to go on the road to give concerts and autographs and stuff like that?"

I cuffed him and made him smile.

"You trying to get rid of me or something? I'm not going anyplace but into that dumb class. When I get a guitar, I'll entertain at Jake's."

"They're raffling one off down at the Youth Center in Northold where Lydia volunteers."

"Wow! Do you think she could fix it so I could win?"

"Pepper!"

"All right. But who else do you know who even wants a guitar, especially someone who has natural talent?"

Then Frankie cuffed *me* and we went into history laughing, which didn't make the teacher overjoyed at our dropping in late.

Eleven

When Pepper gets her teeth into an idea, she holds on like Spot does to my bedroom slipper. Frankly, I wished I had never mentioned that guitar the Northold Youth Center is raffling off. Nothing would do until I made sure Mom was going to take us over there Saturday night, but Mom will go into a coma if Pepper rigs that raffle, and to tell the truth, I am worried sick. Pepper talks as if it is already hers, and as far as I know, she doesn't even have a ticket. Lydia made Mom buy the six she had left, and Mom put Pepper's name on one of them, but all the volunteers had to sell fifty tickets, and most everybody on the North Fork volunteers at the Youth Center.

The Center was packed when we arrived. I knew

Pepper was excited when she didn't even pay much attention to her supper. Oh, she ate all of her fried chicken, and the dark meat Mom didn't want, but I had to remind her about dessert. She ate cherry pie and double fudge cake, but her mind was on that guitar.

When Fallon and Melinda Sue came in with Fallon's parents, Pepper said, "If Fallon wins it, I'll know there is no God."

"What did she say?" Mom's ears always perk up when the Lord's name is mentioned.

"I said, I've been praying to God I'd win that guitar, Mrs. Banning," Pepper said.

"I'm glad to hear you're saying your prayers, Pepper Junior, but we mustn't ask the Lord for material rewards."

"After I have my guitar, I'll spend all my time thanking Him, Mrs. Banning. I promise."

When the drawing started, Pepper was as tight as a bowstring. They let Lydia's youngest daughter, Tracy, reach in the glass bowl for the ticket.

"Charles Carruthers. Is Charles Carruthers in the audience?"

People around us were saying "Who? Oh, that's Chub," but Pepper knew immediately. She shot out of her seat before I could grab her.

"Isn't that nice? Pepper has gone over to congratulate Chub," Mom said.

149

Inside I was groaning, but I sat there while they pulled the tickets for the ten-speed bike and a Linda Ronstadt album. I didn't even want to know what Pepper was saying to Chub, but I couldn't make myself look away. He must have been driving a hard bargain because Pepper was using her hands, counting off on her fingers, and talking a blue streak.

They were working some kind of a deal. Pepper was counting out her money. Chub must not have believed she gave it all to him, because she turned the pocket of her red jacket inside out. I couldn't stand it anymore. When I walked up, Chub was saying, "You'll do all my English themes, even the long ones? And the book reports?"

"All of 'em."

"And I'll be invited to every party you *ever* have?"

"Chub, even my wedding, I promise."

"But I bet I could sell that guitar for more than twenty-five dollars and it wouldn't have to be on the installment plan."

"Look, I already gave you seven dollars and fifty cents, and think of the fringe benefits I've thrown in. Now do we have a deal or what?"

Chub's generosity is not proportioned to his weight. Until she actually had that guitar case in her hands, I wasn't sure Pepper would get the job done. But when she did, I couldn't believe how she carried on. She hugged it and danced around in circles. Even laid her cheek against the case. I don't think she looks at me like that when I kiss her.

"Oh, Frankie, can you believe it? We'll start practicing our act tonight, just as soon as we get home. Do you suppose your Mom's ready to go?" Pepper had her arms around that guitar, clutching it up against her like somebody might try to take it away from her.

"What act?" Chub asked. "Part of the deal is, if you have a group, I get to be in it."

"Chub, can you sing?" Pepper asked.

"Frankie can't either. He didn't even make chorus."

"Look, I'll teach you guys, okay? How do you think Pepper and the Poppers sounds for our name?"

"How about Pepper and the Princes?" Chub said.

"Hey, that's terrific! I can see it in neon." She wrote it in the air and then threw her free arm around my shoulders and pressed her face against mine, right there in the Youth Center in front of my Mom and half the town. Of course, Chub always has to horn in, so he put his face against her other cheek even though she unintentionally hit him in the chin with her guitar case.

"Hold it," Lydia said and she snapped our pictures, which came out in the *Northold Times* the next week.

At first it was okay. Pepper took the guitar to school the next day, of course, and Mr. Staff showed her some chords. By the time I got up to her house that night, she had figured out how to play some songs she and

Granny could sing like "You Are My Sunshine" and "Home on the Range." Pepper said I sounded fine when I sang along, but it seemed to me I was way down below them, especially when we tried "O Little Town of Bethlehem."

I know it sounds stupid to be jealous of a guitar, but all Pepper wanted to do was plunk around on that old thing. She and Granny rigged up a strap, and when she wasn't playing it, she always had it slung over her shoulder.

Another thing that bugged me to death, but did not seem to bother Pepper at all, was Chub always hanging around griping about her making another installment payment. She could only get him off her back by playing him a new song. She seemed to learn one every day. She picked out "The Old Rugged Cross" for Granny and Mom, but Pepper loves the blues. Chub would listen to anything.

When he didn't have a class, Mr. Staff would let her hang out in the band room so he could show her slides and how to develop calluses on her fingers. I used to try to hide the ones I got picking sweet corn. She also listened to records, trying to play along, and would hardly talk to a guy at all. If the band had to practice, Pepper would be in the boiler room with Henry, who tapped his foot and puffed his pipe in time. I don't know how he found the tall stool for her, but he kept it behind the furnace, and that's where she performed for Chub, who never could tell when he wasn't wanted.

Even the night we put up Granny's Christmas tree a little early, Pepper kept talking about jazz being played in only five or six keys, but how you put so much pain in the music it hurt your hands to play it. Any other time, she would have been making a big fuss over the ornaments her grandfather had carved out of soft pine—angels, snowflakes, stars, snowmen, balls with designs around the middle. But she was filled up and running over with excitement about that guitar. Anything Pepper wanted to go on about was okay with Granny. I think, after sitting by that fire alone all those years, Pepper could have talked Chinese and she would have enjoyed it.

At home our tree had a lot more color to it, and the lights blinked at you. Mom puts a lot of work into that tree. She has been collecting ornaments from church bazaars since she was a bride. I think Pepper probably hurt her feelings when she told her the prettiest tree she had ever seen, except for Granny's, was a pink one with bows and sequined apples in a movie star's yard she and Zack had once spotted when they were driving around in Beverly Hills.

Dad always cusses when he tries to put our tree in the stand. Every year. That hurts Mom's feelings too. She tells me he has been trying to ruin Christmas for her that way for thirty-seven years, and I must promise her when I have a family of my own I won't take the Lord's name in vain, especially when it's time to celebrate his birthday. I didn't tell her, but I doubt if my cussing would upset Pepper very much.

The tree Dad takes a lot of pride in is the one they decorate at the top of the main street in town. He and Vic Terry and the other men on the council work for days getting it to look just right. Mom dreads them putting that up like the plague because the last day they always stop off at The Quiet Man to celebrate.

Mom always says the Lord was looking after us because the tragedy happened on the first day they were working on the tree. Dad had come right home and was washing up. I had been home from school for almost an hour and was trying to do my homework so I could go up to Pepper's to work on our Christmas presents. The windows were all shut up, so I didn't hear Pepper until she hit our back porch at a dead run, screaming.

"Mr. Banning, Mr. Banning. Come quick! It's Granny."

By the time I got downstairs, Dad was practically holding her up, and I've never seen anyone look that scared. Her hair was wild like she had been in the wind, her face twisted, and she didn't even have a coat on.

"I couldn't find her. The fire was out, so I knew she'd been gone a long time."

Mom was on the phone and Dad was getting into his coat.

"Will we need an ambulance?" Mom asked.

"Yes, and a stretcher. Something's broke and she's on the beach. I covered her up with my jacket, but I couldn't get her up. It hurts too much."

Pepper was crying and her nose was running. Mom grabbed a box of tissues as we ran out the back door and got in the car.

"I told her not to get wood. There was still some left. She could have made it till I got home."

"There, there, Pepper. It's not your fault, honey. Here, blow your nose."

Dad, Pepper, and I took the lap robe from the car and went to the beach while Mom waited for the ambulance.

The doctor said he couldn't tell if Mis' Marlan had fallen and that had broken her hip, or if it had broken as old people's bones will and that's what made her fall. She was unconscious and couldn't tell us anything.

We stayed at the hospital until they got her hip set and she was back in intensive care, but the doctor finally told us we might as well go on home and get some sleep because she wouldn't know if we were there or not. Dad practically had to carry Pepper out of the hospital. We finally got her to go when Mom promised she would bring her back the first thing in the morning.

All the way home Pepper didn't say a word. She sat hunched over in the corner looking like a pup Lydia's kids had had who they claimed had died of a broken heart because he never got over missing the rest of the litter. When Dad turned into our driveway, she finally sat up.

"Mr. Banning, I have to go home to keep the fire going. Things will freeze."

"I'll go up and bank it till morning, Pepper Junior. Tomorrow we can see what else has to be done."

"We better pick up some clothes for Pepper," I said, feeling guilty about being glad she'd have to stay with us when Granny was so sick and she was so miserable.

Dad drove up to Granny's house and when they came out, all Pepper had was her hairbrush and the guitar over her shoulder. Mom went back and found her toothbrush, clean jeans, a nightshirt, and some underwear. No one thought about tops, so she wore my shirts the rest of the week.

Maybe we were all in a daze, or maybe none of us could stand to think ahead because we never talked about anything beyond the day we were living. Sometimes when I was trying to fall asleep, it was as if there was a radio in my mind making comments about Mis' Marlan really being in bad shape and how health care costs had gotten out of hand, but I always tried to shut it off.

In the mornings we would talk about the things we

could do something about. We would decide if Mom would pick me and Pepper up after school to go to the hospital or if we would go in the evening. When Granny improved so she could talk to us, we would ask her what she had for supper and tell her things that happened at school. Pepper made up some things, but Granny enjoyed her tales so much, even Mom didn't seem to think it mattered much. Sometimes Pepper played the guitar for her, and we took a little Christmas tree that would fit on the top of her bureau. Mom got decorations from the five-and-ten. We left the one with Mr. Marlan's carving intact at Granny's house. Granny and Pepper never mentioned calling Zack. And Mom and Dad only talked about it when they weren't around.

I was all torn up about Granny being sick and worried about what was going to happen to Pepper in the long run, but having Pepper living in our house was great. Mom gave her Ruth's old room, which was at the opposite end of the hall from mine with Mom and Dad's room in between, but while they were downstairs watching television, we had a lot of privacy.

Then one night, to my lasting regret, I pushed my luck. Pepper had gone to take her shower because we could hear the TV news and knew the folks would be coming up when it was over. When I went across the hall to the bathroom, I caught a glimpse of Pepper going into her room wearing one of Betty's Mother

Hubbard gowns Mom had given her. She had her hair tied up on top of her head with a pink ribbon and the steam from the shower had made it curly. I thought she looked like one of those soft squeezable dolls, and I just had to go kiss her goodnight again.

Mom had put white ruffled pillows on Pepper's bed, and she was propped up reading when I came into her room. I sat on the edge of her bed and she put her arms around my neck. She smelled like lemon soap.

"Your Mom will have kittens if she finds you in here," she said, but she didn't let go of me. Then she bit my ear, and I yelped just as we heard Mom on the steps.

"Frankie? Frankie! I'll look at your homework now, young man."

Walking out in that hall and facing my mom was worse than walking the plank could ever have been. She made me feel ashamed about things I hadn't even done. Ruth says Mom was different until Lydia turned out to be such a handful. I wish I had been around then.

We looked over my homework, and she didn't say a word, but the expression on her face let me know I had stabbed her in the heart and it still hurt.

At breakfast she said we would go to the hospital after school because she thought Pepper and I would *want* to go to church with her that night.

When she went in the pantry, Pepper whispered,

"Does her church have confession?" She looked relieved when I shook my head.

Pepper sat between Mom and me straight as a stick until the preacher started reading the passage he was going to preach on. About in the middle, when he really got warmed up, she started leaning forward in her seat, and knowing Pepper, I was hoping she wasn't going to do anything crazy.

" 'And when thou reap the harvest of your land thou shall not make clean riddance of the corner of thy field when thou reapest. Neither shall thou gather any gleaning of thy harvest; thou shall leave them unto the poor and to the stranger.' "

All Pepper did was take hold of my hand so Mom couldn't see, and that wasn't crazy.

"Ladies and gentlemen, we know the beautiful symbolism of the Lord's words. We know that it is not only the farmer who must leave his gleanings, but you and I. All of God's children. And the stranger? We might recognize his face, but not know his heart. There are those who are poor who have job security and money in the bank. The poor in spirit. You might ask, but what do I have to give? All of us have love. But the best gift of all? Hope, my friends, that in these troubled, sinful times is in short supply."

I always feel terrible about it, but my mind usually wanders in church. And holding hands with Pepper made it even worse than usual, but Pepper had her attention riveted on the preacher. Even Mom glanced at her and must have thought she looked like an angel too because she smiled, and I thought maybe she had forgotten about finding me in Pepper's room.

Once, Pepper leaned over and whispered in my ear, "Even Zack left Trenton." Mom grimaced, so I didn't tell her I doubted the preacher was interpreting the scripture that freely. But I wouldn't be surprised if Lydia agreed with Pepper. Trenton *is* her favorite.

"Now, ladies and gentlemen, before we return to the comfort of our homes tonight, let us bow our heads in prayer for our sister, Mrs. Elizabeth Marlan, who is confined in the hospital with a broken hip."

Pepper squeezed my fingers till the blood stopped, and tears rolled into her turtleneck, but she looked proud.

The trouble started the next Sunday when Mis' Marlan's doctor called Dad at home to talk about a whole pack of worries. Since Granny didn't have any health insurance and the government would only pay so much, he wanted to know how the rest of the bill was going to be taken care of. When an old woman is flat on her back, it seems plain cruel to start worrying about money, but the doctor didn't seem to be sensitive to how hard up Pepper and Granny were. What I hoped they wouldn't tell Pepper was how he thought Granny would probably not ever walk again. He and Dad discussed painful things like where they were going to put her so she could get proper care. Seemed like they had people standing in line to take Mis' Marlan's bed away from her at the hospital.

Pepper was taking a shower, so I know she couldn't have heard them, but it's like she sensed what was going on.

At dinner Pepper was quieter than usual. Mom noticed and said, "Pepper, why don't we wrap up a piece of this angel food cake and take it to your grandmother this afternoon?"

"I already have." Pepper held up a piece wrapped in a paper napkin I didn't even know she had in her lap. "I guess I better be talking to the doctor about bringing her home. It's probably costing us a mint, and I can take care of her just fine now that she's so much better."

Mom and Dad exchanged one of their looks, and Dad leaned toward her across the table. "Pepper, Lucille and I were just talking about that this morning, and we were thinking your grandmother might be more comfortable over in the Soundfront Nursing Home. They've got good clean facilities, serve a decent meal, and we know most of the folks who work there."

If he had struck her with the flat of his hand, Pepper couldn't have winced any more.

"She wouldn't want to be away from home. Since I

need to practice my guitar anyway, I've decided to take the rest of this year off from school, and by summer I'll have Granny in good shape."

"You're only fourteen, Pepper. The law says you must go until sixteen, and besides, your grandmother needs professional care, a balanced diet. Lucille and I were just wondering if . . . if you wanted to get in touch with your dad?"

I know suggesting bringing Zack Marlan back to this county must have been awful hard for Dad.

"Well, Zack's pretty tied up in a new enterprise he's working on, so I don't think we have to drag him way out here, not that he wouldn't be on the next bus if we asked him, but Granny and I'll be okay." Pepper wriggled around in her chair like she couldn't find a comfortable way to sit. "And I know about that law, but it takes 'em a while to even find out you're gone, and then they have to get the papers together and find someone to go after you. I've done it before. I think I could probably make it till summer."

Mom looked all teary-eyed and said we didn't have to decide anything right that minute. Seemed to me she was nicer to Pepper all the rest of the day, even asked her to play her guitar after supper. I was feeling miserable myself, like I had a bellyache that wouldn't quit.

The kids at school were all nicer to Pepper too, but frankly, I think they made her feel worse. They didn't

162

act very natural. I guess everybody in Port of Egypt was wondering what was going to happen to Mis' Marlan, probably talking about it at the supper table. Pepper would walk past a group, and they would stop talking and smile at her kind of sicklike, the way you do when you have to make a call at the funeral home when somebody's died. Jeff Porter even said "excuse me" when he bumped her desk coming into English class.

Miss Davis stopped us after class one day and asked Pepper if she could send her grandmother something to read in the hospital.

"I've been reading 'The Outcasts of Poker Flats' to her. She liked that. Maybe when I bring her home, you could give us something else."

"Oh, I didn't know you were planning to bring her home."

"Any day now. I'd like for her to make it before Christmas so we could put the candles on our tree."

"Is your father going to come to help you, Pepper?" Miss Davis asked.

"He wants to, but Granny and I think it would be better for him to stay in California where he can make a lot of money to send us for the doctor bills and everything. I really don't need any help in taking care of her."

Pepper went off to the band room to practice her guitar, but I went back to Miss Davis' room. I didn't know how to talk to her about how bad I was feeling. To tell the truth, I was pissed off at the whole Marlan outfit, even Pepper. Them and their imaginations were fine when it was storytelling time, but someone had to look at Granny's situation straight on or I was afraid I was going to lose Pepper. I stood around fumbling with the books on Miss Davis' desk until she finally helped me out.

"You're worried about Pepper, aren't you Frankie?"

"I'd like to punch Zack Marlan in the nose is what I'd really like to do."

What I did was kick Miss Davis' metal wastepaper basket, and it made a devil of a racket.

"Sorry."

"Is he sending them any money?"

"Not even enough to feed them proper, as far as I can tell. I don't think he writes more than once a month. And I bet a dollar Pepper hasn't even told him about Granny being sick. What's wrong with her, Miss Davis? Why can't she ever be sensible and see things the way they really are?"

"Pepper's a survivor, Frankie. I imagine she had to learn the hard way. It seems to me she always knows the truth, but Pepper's a wise kid. She only puts as much on her plate as she can swallow at one time."

"But she won't even be fifteen until March. I've been trying to think of a way to ask my folks if she could live with us forever, but I'm such a bloody coward with my dad."

"I used to be tongue-tied around mine too. We still aren't at ease when we try to discuss my marrying Dan."

Kids were starting to come in for the next class, so I had to go, but I hated to leave Miss Davis. She was the only person I had been able to tell how worried I was. I had gotten used to talking to Pepper about things, and I felt lost. There was always Lydia, but with her and the Marlans, things got complicated. She wasn't any more realistic about Zack than Pepper and Granny.

Mr. O'Brien called Pepper after school that day, offering to buy Granny's five acres again. He said he had put the offer in a letter, but he told her the figure. When I heard how much he was willing to pay, I thought our problems were almost solved. But actually that made things more complicated than before.

For one thing, I began to feel like an intruder in my own house. All the rest of that week, every time I came into a room, I would find Mom and Dad or Mom and Lydia in a huddle, but the moment they caught sight of me, they would say something stupid like asking me if I wanted a glass of milk, even if I had just finished a meal.

I learned if I'd walk soft and stand outside a door,

sometimes I could pick up the drift of what was going on. Like when I heard Mom tell Dad that Pepper and I were getting to that "age" and there was no way Pepper could live with us unless he wanted a "Lydia situation" on his hands.

Dad said, "Lucille, if you're telling me my choice is another Marlan bastard or a hundred and fifty condos in my backyard, I'm going down to The Quiet Man and drink my supper."

Then he saw me and asked why in the hell I wasn't shelling the popcorn, which he hadn't even told me to do.

Lydia stopped in to see Mis' Marlan when she was volunteering as a candy striper at the hospital. Afterward, I overheard Mom saying, "Now, Lydia, for once in your life, you must listen to me. You've got a good life, a nice family, and a husband who adores you, but even Harvey Millbock is only going to put up with so much, and don't you forget it. That man has already acted like a saint. No matter what you say, he has tried real hard with Trenton. And we all know what a pistol that boy can be!"

"Comes by it honestly. Just like his dad, right, Mom?" Lydia said.

"All you need to do to drive Harvey straight into the arms of another woman is to bring Pepper Junior Marlan into your home. Then where would you be, my girl? You have to think of your own children."

166

Lydia laughed and said, "Maybe I could get a guitar and Pepper and I could work up an act."

But I didn't hear her mention taking Pepper home with her anymore. I can see how having Trenton and Pepper in the same house could be a trial for Harvey but surely we all weren't going to abandon Pepper like she was a stray dog that had wandered into the neighborhood. I had never been so miserable in my life.

Pepper had lost her bounce too. Since she didn't have any better ideas about solving the problem than I did, we tried to talk about other things, but it was like trying to ignore a drought when the plants all around you were dying.

Pepper spent more and more time up at Granny's house, even though there wasn't any heat and Dad had blocked the flue on the fireplace. I worried about her freezing to death, but she'd take her guitar and go up there to think, I guess.

Twelve

The way I have it figured, there is just so much happiness. Not enough to go around for everyone to have some all the time, so it's divvied up so most people get a little a part of the time. Like when I met Frankie and got my own guitar. If every yo-yo in the world were happy all the time, probably nothing would ever get done. Nobody would have any hustle.

It doesn't do a bit of good trying to figure out what Granny has done to deserve being in such a bad fix, other than getting old. When my grandfather was alive she said they had a high old time, going to dances and him making their furniture and always carving pretty things for her like her jewelry box where she keeps Zack's letters. The Marlans are better artists than

168

farmers, Granny says, but artists are more fun she thinks. Since I've got this artistic heritage, I suppose it was just meant for me to be a famous guitar player. Granny thinks there is no doubt about it.

When I get around to it, I've got to ask that doctor how much Granny and I owe over at the hospital. I thought I would concentrate on getting her back to good health, and then I would begin to work on a way to pay off the bill. I practice all the time because I know a good guitar player can make a bundle.

That day when I found Granny on the beach, so cold and hurting till it like to broke my heart, I promised her if she would just hang on until I could get help, she would never have to worry about anything again because I would always take care of her. And I'm going to, no matter what it takes.

The only good thing to come out of Granny's illness is me owning my guitar free and clear. Chub came up to me a few days after she got hurt and said, "My mom says since your grandmother is dying, I shouldn't make you pay the other installments on the guitar."

"Granny'll dance at your wedding, Chub Carruthers, but your mom's got a good idea about the guitar. We're going to need all of our money to pay her bills. I'll write out a bill of sale."

"Why're you going to do that, if you're not paying me anything?"

"What I'm paying you is called goodwill. Don't you

know anything, Chub? Sign right here at the bottom by the date."

I keep the paper explaining our deal in my guitar case, just in case Chub has any ideas about changing his mind when he finds out Granny is going to be just fine.

Fallon O'Brien's dad sent me a message too, but Granny and I aren't in bad enough straits to be going to the O'Briens for help. That family has pretty much confirmed what I picked up traveling around with Zack about sleeping with one eye open.

Fallon and I have gym class together, and she hung around the other day while I was drying my hair after the shower. I was trying to brush out the curl the steam always makes. She came up behind me and talked to my image in the mirror.

"I like your hair that way, Pepper Junior."

"This is the same way I always wear it."

"Well, I guess it's because you just look so much better than when you first got here. Cleaner, and more . . . more All-American, you know?"

I knew if I pulled every hair off her head, Spike would give me detention and I couldn't look after Granny, so I controlled myself, but I'm not about to forget I owe her one.

"California's not exactly the Third World, but of course, you wouldn't know anything about a sophisticated place like that since you've had to live out here with the farmers."

"Pepper, I don't know why you always have to be snooty. I'm trying to be your friend. Since your grandmother's so sick and you're so poor, my parents thought I should be extra nice to you."

"Thanks, Fallon, but I've already seen what a good friend you can be, remember?"

"Well, if you're talking about that silly crush I had on Donnie Carruthers, you can forget it. I've learned my lesson about wild older boys."

I raised my eyebrow at her reflection in the mirror and went right on brushing my hair.

"I guess you think I should have told Mr. Spade that getting in the car was my idea?"

I just went on brushing my hair, but the mirror was showing Fallon blushing as if she'd painted her cheeks. I let her stew, but I couldn't figure out what Fallon wanted. I had seen that girl in the trenches, and she couldn't convince me she was just concerned about Granny's health.

"I'm sorry, Pepper Junior. I was just so scared since I had never been in trouble before."

"Trouble strengthens your character."

"I know you have trouble now, and my daddy would like to help you."

I just bet he would.

"Since you're staying with the Bannings, he couldn't talk to you himself, but he said if I would just mention to you how concerned my family is about your situation . . . and maybe find out who your lawyer is. . . ."

"My lawyer? The worst scrape I've been in since I've been here was taking a ride with your boyfriend. Why would I need a lawyer?"

"Someone will have to represent your interests when you sell your grandmother's waterfront property. Surely, even *you* know that."

"Listen, Fallon, you be sure to thank your dad for being so concerned about my grandmother's health, will you? But you tell him she'll be coming home in a few days, and if we're in the mood for company this summer, maybe we'll ask you and your folks out to swim on our beach."

"I don't know why I even bothered trying to be nice to you, Pepper Marlan. Like my mother says, all Daddy has to do is call your father in California. You're not old enough to sign anything anyway."

I wanted to hit her! I've never wanted to pound anyone to powder so badly in my life. Why in the hell couldn't she just leave me alone? My eyes were burning, but if she thought I was going to let her make me cry, she was crazy. If I was able to hold the tears back until the Bannings were asleep at night, I wasn't going to break down in front of Fallon O'Brien.

"Listen, Fallon, you take a message to your dad for

me. You tell him to keep his nose out of my business. When I need him, I'll call him, and tell him not to hold his breath."

"You're impossible! You always have been."

Fallon turned and strutted out of there as if she were the drum majorette with the band. When she got to the door, I said, "And for your information, my dad always winters in Tahiti and can't be reached by phone."

I could have added that I would ask her parents out to swim if they hadn't got a divorce by then, but I didn't want to stoop to her level.

The one thing about Granny and me is that we don't need a lot of words to understand the way the other one is thinking. We hit it off that way right from the start. When I got off the bus and walked up that road to her house the first day, I was planning an elaborate story to tell her about why I had come. She took one look at me, wrapped her bony old arms around me, and I knew I didn't need the story. She wanted me.

Frankie wasn't with me when I told her I had written Zack to tell him about her accident. Even though Frankie and I are planning on getting married in about ten years, there are still some things about our family that he doesn't understand. After he meets Zack, it will be easier to explain. With so many other problems to deal with, I didn't see any reason to go into a lot of detail. Besides, Granny and I've got a shorthand that makes us able to understand each other real easy.

"Granny, you know how Zack is. If I had told him you were going to be laid up for a while, he would have jumped on the first bus out of Oakland. Left his new enterprise and everything, so I just told him I brought you in to get checked over," I told her.

"You did the right thing, child. No use to worry my boy. You and I can take care of things that need to be done," she said.

Zack sent her a Hallmark card. She has the rest of her cards from Miss Davis, the preacher, and everyone on the chest under her Christmas tree, but she has the newspaper picture of Chub, Frankie, and me and Zack's card on her bedside table. There are a bunch of colorful flowers on the front and it says "Get Well Wishes for My Loving Mother." He signed it "Lots of Love from Your Son Zack" with a red pen.

Granny might be right about the Marlan men being artistic. Grandpa sure did make some super furniture, but Zack hasn't seemed to have found his talent yet. Anyway, with the problems we've got now, what we need is a magician, not an artist. I'm afraid it's up to us.

Being so worried about Granny, I had lost my spirit for Christmas, but I hoped the Bannings were still into it in a big way. Every time Frankie and I came home, they were in a huddle, but they'd break it up when they saw us. Since I had a feeling I wouldn't like anything they might be planning for Granny and me, I told myself they were talking about surprises to go under the tree and I better finish up my presents. Spending so much time at the hospital, I worried about not having had time to finish the tie rack I was making out of driftwood for Mr. Banning.

I got my surprise the weekend before Christmas. Saturday morning Frankie's dad left early in the truck. Mrs. Banning fussed and bustled around all morning not accomplishing much of anything, as far as I could tell. She made a pie crust and forgot the salt. About eleven o'clock when she got the vacuum cleaner out and started on the living room carpet she had swept right after breakfast, Frankie and I suggested maybe she would like to read her Bible for a while. We told her we would fix lunch, since the state she was in, no telling what she would have done to the hamburgers we were having.

Usually Mrs. Banning finds a lot of comfort in her Bible, but I could tell she was having as much trouble concentrating as I do when I try to read my science assignment. Seemed to me her eyes followed me everywhere I went. At lunch, she kept insisting I eat more. After pizza, hamburgers are my favorite food, but I had already had three and we made them the size of Big Macs.

When we got to the hospital, Mr. Banning was already there. I knew something was up. Granny reached out her arms to me when I came in the door and hugged me the way she usually does when I leave.

I hugged her back, but then I looked at Mr. Banning and said, "What's going on around here?"

"Pepper, Frank and that nice Dr. Stone got me into a wheelchair this morning and drove me in the hospital van over to the Soundfront Nursing Home."

"You're not going there!"

I felt as if someone had dropped a bank safe on my chest.

"It's real nice, honey. My room would look right out on the water. I could watch the gulls."

"We do that at home."

"But over there I'd be sharing my room with Minnie Butler. We knew each other when we were girls. And we'd have a TV, so I could watch that Donahue fellow you've been telling me about."

"You told me Minnie Butler had a stroke. I can take care of you better at home, and Frankie and I are working on getting you a TV."

"Pepper Junior, we are all proud of you for wanting to take care of your grandmother, but you wouldn't be able to do it up there by yourself, even with the help of the Lord," Mrs. Banning said.

"I can! And over there, they'll charge . . ."

"Before I tell you the plan your grandmother and I

have been talking about, I think it's only right for me to tell you there has been another offer," Mr. Banning said.

"If you're talking about Mr. O'Brien, forget it. I don't want to do business with them."

"Don't make too hasty a judgment, Pepper. You better read what he has to say first." Mr. Banning handed me a piece of paper.

I ran my finger across the letters in the name across the top of the page. They stood off the paper about a foot. I should have expected the O'Briens to be showy, even in a letter. What he said was smooth as oil. Then a sentence jumped off the page at me. "Selling your property as a site for one hundred and fifty luxury condominiums for vacation/leisure homes could put you and your family on easy street. . . ."

"It's no secret that I don't cotton to summer people lollygagging around here in their pink pants held up with Gucci belts, and O'Brien claims he has the votes to get his condos approved," Mr. Banning said. "I don't believe it, but I'm not willing to take the chance of having the fumes from a hundred and fifty barbeque parties floating in my windows next summer. So here's what I've offered your grandmother."

"What about Pepper?" Frankie asked, but his dad ignored him, and his mother started twisting her rings.

"I'll buy the five acres, put the capital to work in a trust fund to be used to pay your grandmother's expenses here at the hospital and whatever it costs over at the Soundfront. At her death if there is anything left, it will go toward your education. If the fund is used up before Mrs. Marlan's death, I've written into the contract that I will be responsible for her care as long as she lives."

"You stop talking like that! Granny's going to be fine."

"We're just thinking of the future, Pepper. Now, it's only fair to tell you that O'Brien is offering you more up-front money. Your grandmother is leaving the decision up to you, but you might want to talk this over with your . . . dad."

I darted a quick look at Granny. As usual we didn't need the words. She knew like I did that there was no use tempting Zack with a shortcut to easy street when we could handle everything ourselves.

"My father's just going into a new partnership, and he's awful busy. There's no reason to take up his time with things Granny and I can manage on our own. Right, Granny?"

Granny's smile was so sweet. "That's right, Pepper Junior. You're a smart girl. You'll do just fine."

I knew my voice was sounding funny, but I felt like I had swallowed a beach ball and it was blowing up bigger and bigger, taking all my wind. But there were a few things we had to settle.

"I want some other things written into that contract. Like you have to promise not to tear down our house."

"Okay. We'll plant the truck patch, but the house sits on a pretty rocky piece anyway, and we'd have to clear all those trees."

A picture of our house sitting there with the wind blowing through the pines flashed through my mind, and for a minute my throat closed up. If I thought about the Christmas tree with Grandpa's ornaments waiting for us to put on the candles, I knew I was going to start crying and never stop. I had to put it out of my mind. Frankie and his mom were shedding enough tears for all of us.

"And I want it to say I can buy it back as soon as I get the money together."

Mr. Banning nodded.

"You know, Granny, even Mr. Staff thinks it's not going to be any time at all until I'm good enough on the guitar to be making a mint. Then we'll go home and hire a nurse to look after you when I have to go to Europe on tour and things like that."

"Sure we will honey."

"Then we have a deal?" Mr. Banning said. He stuck out his hand.

"You're going to have to put your faith in the Lord, Pepper Junior," Mrs. Banning said.

Frankie's mom means well, but it was her husband

I was going to have to put my faith in, and I wasn't used to handing my fate over to anyone else. The hardest thing I ever did was shake his hand.

The next hardest thing I ever did was prepare myself to leave. Traveling around with Zack, I had had lots of experience with moving on, but this was something different. Zack and I traveled light, could pack up everything and carry it with us. What I'd found here, I couldn't take with me. It was different with a home. And even though it was only for a short time, I couldn't help but worry about Granny being so old. And Frankie? Well, I didn't know what he was going to do without me. If I didn't tell him all the time that he wasn't a noodle, he let people walk all over him. I still can't understand why he doesn't realize he's the best there is. I don't know what I'm going to do without him either.

But thoughts like that were never going to help me do what I had to do.

Shoot, I knew I could have stayed with the Bannings or Lydia if I had wanted to, but like I told Frankie, most of the guitar players get their start in California. Besides, since I know his parents were probably wishing I would stay, I didn't want to tell him I wouldn't feel right about it. Like Granny and I always say, the Marlans never lose their pride. Even when Zack and I have been doing hard time, we never took charity. Granny hasn't either.

Granny and I were really impressed with what a nice job they did on her room over at the Soundfront. I told her it was like being in a fancy resort, having her own bathroom and a view of the water. Minnie Butler's not going to be any problem at all. She doesn't even know where she is and can't say a word. So Granny will get to watch whatever TV programs she wants with no static from Minnie. Since it's only temporary until I can get back here and we can go home, she'll be just fine. When I told her Frankie and I would be getting married before she knew it, and we had already decided we wanted to live with her because she made such good gingerbread, we both stopped crying, and she laughed like she used to before she got hurt.

We tried to pretend Christmas was just a normal holiday. For a joke Lydia had put a frozen pizza under the tree for me. When everyone else went home and Frankie's folks went up to bed, we heated it up. I think I must have been coming down with a sore throat though because I couldn't even swallow it, so we went in and lay down on the couch. I promised Frankie I'd write him every day, and I must have promised him a dozen times that Rocky Rivers could disappear for all I cared. Like I told him, Zack would probably be ready to split with old Bea by the time I got to Oakland and we'd be moving on. Away from Bea *and* Rocky Rivers. Maybe down around LA where I could get my start. I'd find us a place on the beach. Of course, it wouldn't be as good as Granny's. Nothing could be. I'd only be working down there to buy Granny's house back. But with so little time left, I didn't even want to think about what it would be like in California. Mainly Frankie and I just held each other and wished the clock wouldn't move so fast.

The day after Christmas, I got my things all packed into Lydia's duffle bag and put my guitar over my shoulder, but Mr. and Mrs. Banning were still arguing when we got in the car. You would never have known I was sitting right there in the backseat holding onto Frankie's hand the way they were carrying on.

"Frank, I tell you it's not Christian to put a fourteen-year-old girl on a Greyhound bus and expect her to find her way to Oakland, California. I don't care what she says."

I had told her a dozen times I had found my way to Port of Egypt, and it wasn't even on the map.

"Now, Lucille, you know I offered to buy her a plane ticket, but she insisted on taking the bus."

Since I have never been on a plane, I was tempted to take him up on his offer until I found out how much it cost. Granny's TV costs ten dollars a week, and I wanted to be sure she could have it for company until I got back. Besides, I don't know what the odds are on planes going down, and all our plans hinge on me

182

getting to California and becoming a famous guitar player. I couldn't take the chance.

When we got to the place on the highway where the jitney that would take me to the New York bus station stops, Mrs. Banning gave me a Bible I didn't have room for and kept telling me to button up my jacket so I wouldn't get sick. They were going to let Frankie wait for the jitney with me while they went into the post office, which I thought was considerate of them, but I was beginning to think we weren't going to have any time alone at all.

Finally Mr. Banning said, "Lucille, leave the girl alone. You've buttoned her jacket four times already."

Then he turned to me. "Pepper Junior, I don't want you to worry about your grandmother. I'll look after her."

I believed him. When he stuck out his hand, this time I took it without thinking.

They left Frankie and me standing on the shoulder of the highway, in front of a potato field, of course. He sure had changed since that day I winked at him and he turned red as a fire engine. He put his arms around me right there on the road and buried his face in my hair.

"Pepper Junior, I don't know how I'm going to make it without you."

I felt the same way, but it would only hurt worse if

I admitted it. Over his shoulder I could see what was left of a gleanings pile. A few frozen potatoes no one had picked up. I remembered the preacher saying the best thing you could leave anybody was hope.

"Don't you worry, Frankie, I'll come back to get you when we grow up."